I0831342

Point Guard

a novel

by Victor Pearn

Pearn and Associates, Inc.

Published by Pearn & Associates, Inc., Boulder, Colorado
For general information about our other products and services please contact us at (720) 406-8858.

Cover design by Terence Orin at Colorado Art & Design Company, 502 Sugarloaf Road, Boulder, CO 80302. Phone (303) 444-0567.

Library of Congress Control Number: 2006900141

Pearn, Victor, 1950
Point Guard / by Victor Pearn. 1st ed.

ISBN 0-9777318-0-4 (cloth)
1. Basketball 2. Sports History 3. Illinois High School

Printed in the United States of America

Inspired by true events

POINT GUARD

In 1950 Gary was on his way home walking up Southeast Street minding his own business. He had spent the afternoon at the swimming pool and was carrying his wet trunks wrapped in a towel. Three boys on red bicycles with fat tires came screeching up behind him. They jumped off their bikes. Two boys grabbed his arms from behind while the third, a boy named Ronny Jay pounded and pummeled Gary in the stomach with his fists until Gary's eyes rolled up under his eyelids and he slumped over in the ditch.

A couple of minute's later Gary opened his eyes and got up. Although he would be sore for a few days, except for a deeply bruised ego, he was relatively unharmed. Gary picked himself up and looked around. Missing were his wet swimming trunks and the towel they were wrapped in. Also, when he put his hand in his pocket he noticed the change that had been there, less than a dollar, was gone. He shrugged his shoulders and began walking home. He lived a little over a mile away from the swimming pool. The pool was located on the southeastern edge of his hometown Elm City, Illinois.

That was the first time Gary met Ronny Jay. They would run into each other many times as they grew older in a city with a population of less than twenty thousand that was little more than a large farming community. Ronny Jay had an early start on becoming the town bully of his generation. He was destined to be Gary's nemesis.

The sky was clear and it was a beautiful day in the second week of June. As Gary walked home he became angrier and angrier and he told himself he would never let that boy, or anybody else beat him at anything again.

"I may be smaller than they are, but the fight inside of me is going to be bigger and tougher than theirs."

As soon as Gary got home he told his mom everything that happened. Gary was eleven years old and he lived with his mom, two older sisters, a younger sister and a newborn baby brother who was only two months old. Gary's parents were divorced and their dad, a farm worker, lived sixteen miles away in Ashland. Gary rarely saw his dad and Gary's mom hardly ever saw her monthly ten dollar child support payments.

For the next few days after Gary was pounded on by Ronny Jay he did not act like the normally happy guy he usually was. He seemed down in the dumps and that bothered his mom. She knew that Gary was athletic and loved sports so she saved her tips from her waitress job at Elm City Café and purchased a genuine professional basketball for him from the local sporting goods shop.

That did the trick. Where ever Gary went from that day forward he was dribbling his basketball, and grinning from ear-to-ear, and Gary forgot about his incident with Ronny Jay. Gary's family lived on the second floor in a one room flat just off the town square. Even though Gary was a southpaw, he spent countless hours dribbling up and down the stairs to his flat until he became as he used to say, "ambidextrous" and was equally proficient at dribbling with both hands.

This was in stark contrast to Ronny's family that was in the upper strata of Illinois society. Ronny's parents lived on one of the largest pieces of property in the southwestern corner of town. Their farm stretched from the city limits to as far as the eye could see across the southwest prairie. His dad also owned and managed the largest auto distributorship in central Illinois. They were the wealthiest family in Elm City. Ronny's dad had a private indoor basketball court built just for Ronny so that he could practice anytime he wanted.

I'm Gary's brother, the one telling you this story, oh and by the way, all of it is true. It's what really happened way back in the fifties. This is the powerful story of how my brother Gary Pearn dreamed of becoming a star guard on a varsity basketball team; and how he became one of the premier athletes that ever played high school basketball in Illinois. It all began just the way I said with Gary walking home from the swimming pool in 1950.

In 1951 the Korean War was more than ruffling the feathers of the American military establishment. Men, who had survived World War I & II, were being used to battle the North Koreans. All of the U.S. military branches were scrambling to find men who could fight. For the first time in history the United States Marine Corps drafted men. Not only did they draft men, they lowered their standards. Before a guy had to be at least six feet tall and weigh 160 pounds to enlist in the Marines. During Korea the Marines took anybody, fat, skinny and short boys too.

What all this had to do with Gary and his basketball dream will become clear a little later....

In 1951 Ernie Hoff, a little guy, graduated from Western, a small University in Illinois. Ernie was five feet four inches tall and weighed only 124 pounds. Ernie's degree was in physical ed. and he excelled in those sports that didn't demand height like wrestling, gymnastics, and being a guard on the basketball team. In fact Ernie lettered all four years in those three sports.

On the day Ernie graduated he received his draft notice from Uncle Sam. On the first day of August he had to go down to St. Louis where he was scheduled to be inducted into the Army. When Ernie walked in, a Marine Sergeant was there asking for Volunteers. That was how the Marines drafted guys. They intercepted them as they were being called into the Army and asked them politely if they would prefer to come on board with the Marines. That was how Ernie Hoff became a Marine.

One week earlier the first group of Marine draftees had landed at MCRD for boot camp in San Diego. The base was like a stirred up hornets nest. The enlisted Marines, those fighting men that had measured up to the original physical standards, did not like the idea of having guys that didn't in their ranks.

Ernie was in the second platoon of draftees to be trained at MCRD. It was a difficult time. The war was raging, and few could stand the rigorous physical exertion the old Marine Corps Drill Instructors were constantly demanding of the draftees.

Ernie, who could always do physical exercises longer and better than anybody else when he was at the university, began to excel in USMC boot camp. All three of his DI's loved him. They made him the platoon leader and put him in for a promotion. He mastered calisthenics so well they used him to demonstrate technique to other platoons.

As soon as his promotion to PFC came in they put him up for another promotion so that by the time he graduated from boot camp he was awarded a set of dress blues that were traditionally given the best Marine in the platoon, and he had been promoted to Lance Corporal. They sent in his promotion for Corporal the day he graduated, and then sent him home for thirty days leave.

In 1952 the war in Korea was still raging and the Marines were still looking for a few good men. When Ernie Hoff returned from leave he found the Marines had changed his draft status to permanent regular, which meant they could make him a Drill Instructor. DI school was twice as long as and more difficult than boot camp. On his first day in school he was excused early to report to the USMC Wrestling team, and he was promoted to Corporal.

Ernie was promoted to Sergeant the day he graduated from DI school and he had the distinction of being the first person to become a DI right out of boot camp. The Wrestling team made him a player-coach. When they found out what an excellent coach he was they made him their football, basketball and track coach as well.

Ernie split his time equally between being a DI and Coaching. He gained invaluable experience training alongside of several world class athletes who, a short time later competed in the Olympic Games for the USA. Near the end of 1952 paperwork to promote Sgt. Ernie Hoff to Staff Sergeant was in process. Because he was drafted they could only keep Ernie two years. The Marine Recruiters tried to promote Ernie before his two year obligation ended in an attempt to persuade him to re-up. Famous for their fighting, not for processing paperwork, the Marines fumbled Ernie's promotion to Staff Sergeant and he decided to get out.

In August, 1953 Gary Pearn submitted to the High School Office his doctor's physical and paperwork signed by his mother giving her son permission to participate in Athletics. They asked him to hand carry copies of his paperwork over to the head basketball coach. The first thing Gary did his freshman year was walk from the school's Main Office over to Coach Quinn's office.

When Gary went in he smiled and handed the coach the paperwork. Coach Quinn scowled at Gary, "What position do you want to try out for?" He handed Gary a clipboard.

"Guard Sir!" Gary said trying to be polite.

"Put your name and position you're trying out for on that list. Are you a ball handler, or a shooter?" Coach Quinn asked.

"I'm a real good ball handler. I'm ambidextrous." Gary said.

“Then sign the list and write Point Guard beside your name.” Coach Quinn said.

“A...Coach there are three different team sheets here...” Gary said.

“Yeah, Frosh, JV and Varsity, put your name down for the team you are trying out for. I make the roster assignments after tryouts.” Coach Quinn said.

Gary wrote his name down for Varsity Basketball and wrote in “Point Guard” for the position he wanted to play. While Gary was writing the Coach read Gary’s paperwork.

“Doesn’t your dad like basketball? I noticed his signature isn’t on the permission slip.” Coach Quinn said.

“I live with my mom Sir. My dad is in Ashland and they’re divorced.” Gary said.

“You’re from a broken family? That’s too bad. It’s going to be tough for you to make it on my team. Boys I have on my teams are all from good families. Their parents are well established in the community. There’s no harm in trying out for the team. Just don’t set your expectations too high.” Coach Quinn said frowning.

Coach Quinn handed Gary a sheet of paper that had the date, time and the place where tryouts were held. Gary took the paper folded it into his pocket and said, “Thank you Sir,” and left his office.

In August 1953, Ernie Hoff returned home to Illinois with an honorable discharge from the USMC. Knowing only that the Marine Corps was not the place for him; he went to see his dad. Everyday in Korea young men who he had trained were fighting and dying and that thought weighed heavily on his mind. Ernie’s dad said, "Son, why don't you stay here and relax and recuperate? I know you love hunting and fishing; we can go hunting and fishing together when I have time. In a few months something will come to you. When the time is right, then you'll know what you want to do."

So for nearly a year Ernie went duck hunting and he went on fishing trips with his dad. He drew unemployment checks, relaxed and enjoyed living at home, with his parents. He slept peacefully every night exactly where he had grown up, in his own bedroom. Life was easy for Ernie Hoff.

At tryouts Gary performed remarkably well; he jumped 38 inches in his vertical leap; clearly he had the best dribbling skills on the court; and he had speed. He demonstrated the ability to pass the ball without looking during his scrimmages. Gary came in first in every across the court sprint drill. He shot free throws well making three out of four of them. Gary's left handed overhead jump shot was a thing of beauty to see. He would leap over three feet in the air and hang up there with his legs tucked underneath him and release the ball with a reverse spin and hit nothing but net.

On the final day of tryouts at the end Coach Quinn told them he liked what he saw in tryouts and they would find the team rosters posted outside his office on Monday morning. Then Gary went into the locker room to shower and change. He felt good about his chances to earn a place on one of the team rosters because he had done his very best.

Just out of the shower, standing in front of his locker, minding his own business, pulling on his white jockey shorts Gary heard a loud POP! He felt searing lightning sharp pain in his buttocks.

"Pearn you worm. Last time I saw you, you were crawling in a ditch." Ronny Jay said laughing. He held the wet towel in his hands that he had snapped Gary with.

The surprise and shock made Gary lose his balance and crash face first into the locker. The protruding handle caught Gary in his right eyebrow causing a gash and immediate swelling. Slightly dazed Gary pulled on his shorts and wiped the blood from his brow.

Inexorable, Gary flew at Ronny and tackled him. Gary's left shoulder landed perfectly against Ronny's upper thighs, and Gary wrapped both arms around the back of his knees and Ronny fell backwards smashing the back of his head against the brown metal locker raising a loud clatter.

Coach Quinn came rushing out of his office to see what the ruckus was just in time to see Gary standing over Ronny. Gary leveled a powerful roundhouse left hook connecting with Ronny's nose, and the Coach was too far away to prevent it. Coach Quinn winced at the loud sound made by Ronny's broken nose. He grabbed Gary around the neck and pulled him away from Ronny.

"Ow, Ow, you broke my nose." Ronny whined, holding his hands on his face leaning his head back.

"Ronny let's get you down to First Aid right now." Coach Quinn said picking Ronny up off the floor.

"Don't think this is over Pearn." Ronny said.

"Pearn I want to see you in my office as soon as you get dressed," Coach Quinn said as he put his arm around Ronny's shoulder walking him down to get help.

Gary was amazed by his own courage. Ronny outweighed him by at least fifty-five pounds and was three inches taller than he was. Ronny was also a year older than Gary. The reason they were both freshmen vying for a position on the basketball team was that Ronny had been held back in the fifth grade. Ronny and Gary had not seen each other because Ronny's parents were Lutherans and he had gone to a Lutheran school from kindergarten through the eighth grade.

By the time Gary dressed his right eye was swollen and turning purple. When Gary went into the office Coach Quinn asked with a grimace, "What have you got to say for yourself?"

Gary didn't say anything.

"You're a damned good guard, but you're from a broken family and you have behavior issues. I have to put you on the team—you're that good, but pull anything like this again and I'll kick you off so fast your head will swim." Coach Quinn snarled.

"I'm sorry Sir! This will never happen again." Gary said.

"You make sure it doesn't." Coach Quinn said.

By Monday Gary's eye was black and he had a scab that ran vertical from an inch above his eyebrow to an inch below his eye on his right cheekbone. There was a welt on his buttocks the shape of an S. Ronny Jay had white tape across his nose. Gary was happy because he found his name on the Junior Varsity roster as the starting guard.

Coach Quinn put Ronny Jay on the roster list as a starting guard on the Varsity not because he was a better player than Gary, but because he was older, six feet tall and weighed 200 pounds. Most likely the main reason the Coach put Ronny on the Varsity team was that his father Ronald Jay was a prominent businessman in the community. In fact, all the kids on the Elm City Varsity were from well established families.

In 1953 Gary's freshman year, he started every game the JV played. The JV lost only four times. They had a winning season. They lost only one game on their home floor. Gary was a fantastic playmaker and he scored more points than any other player on the team. He also did better than any other Varsity player. Unfortunately, that season the Varsity lost more games than they won.

Chapter 2

In 1954 in the summer Ernie Hoff went over to Western University, his alma mater and found a job announcement he liked posted on the bulletin board in the Physical Education Department. Ashland High School was looking to hire a new Coach for Varsity and Junior Varsity Basketball, Baseball and Track. The announcement said to contact Mr. Bruno Bierman at the Board meeting. Mr. Bierman was the Superintendent for Ashland High School.

Ernie went to the Board meeting and talked with Mr. Bierman. In August of 1954 Ernie Hoff was hired as the Head Coach for Ashland High School. He was given a full schedule of classes to teach in addition to his coaching duties. Ashland was a poor tiny farm community in Central Illinois. There were only around 100 students in their entire high school. The kids that went there were unique because they were all friends. They had all grown up playing together their whole lives and they all knew every nuance and character quirk of everybody in school. They helped each other on their farms and with their school work.

One of Ernie's classes was study hall. It was held in the same room where there was a stage. It was the room they used for every important school event like Prom Dances and Graduation Ceremonies. On the walls around the room were glossy black and white photographs of Graduation Classes dating all the way back to 1880. Gary Pearn's mother had been in the Graduating Class of 1930 and at that time her name was Dee Weaver. Gary's dad Forrest Pearn went to school there with his mom, but like most farm boys, he dropped out after the eighth grade to help work on the farm and never went back to school.

In study hall there were four long rows of desks running from the front of the room to the back. Freshmen sat in one long row, sophomores in the next, then juniors, and then seniors. It was a reasonably simple job for Ernie to make sure they were quiet and studying. It was a big change from being a Drill Instructor. Ernie had a passion for his new job, especially for the coaching aspect of it.

His new Varsity basketball team was made up of a highly talented group of sophomores. The team Captain was a junior point guard. When Ernie met the team he was impressed with their athleticism. What gave them a great foundation was the fact that they had all grown up playing together and knew each other's moves. Ernie felt excited about the possibilities of applying the coaching skills he had honed in the Marines to this group of young men. Also, he was excited about teaching the individual training techniques he had learned from some of the best American world class Olympic athletes while he was in the Marines. He thought it would take about a year, but by then he would have a very competitive team.

Ernie noticed that there were Trophies in the display case at Ashland High School that dated up to 1949. He found that the previous coach had dropped the Ashland Tournament. He started the wheels in motion to bring it back. He found three area Varsity teams that would commit to playing in the Tournament at Ashland in December so after a six year hiatus The Ashland Tournament was resumed.

Coach Hoff put his basketball teams through some interestingly vigorous training workouts. There were approximately twenty boys, combining Varsity and Junior Varsity that came to the basketball team practices. There were so few kids that Ernie didn't have any tryouts. Anybody that showed up and made it through his rigorous training program would be on the team.

Coach Hoff was also strict with discipline, anybody he caught smoking would be kicked off the team. He expected them to dress sharp wearing suits to games. They had to all wear their uniforms the same with knee length socks and knee pads, and he preferred that they wear their hair in a flattop that was the raging style most athletes wore back then.

For the first two weeks of practice nobody could touch a basketball. All they did was calisthenics and run. They did a moderate combination of football, wrestling, gymnastics and Marine Corps exercises, which Ernie had put together to try and get them into better physical condition. And he made them run. He made them do both speed and distance workouts. The team liked to whine and grumble about the physical conditioning because they didn't really know what the end results would be, but they couldn't complain too much, Coach Hoff did all the calisthenics with them and he ran with them too. That season the members of his basketball team found themselves in the best physical condition of their young lives. And they were on their way to having their first winning season in basketball for the past ten years.

Ernie turned out to be the perfect Coach for Ashland. He was always doing little things behind the scenes that nobody knew about. He did things that improved the entire school and community. He went out and asked local businesses if they would give money to the athletic department in exchange for poster advertising space on the walls inside the basketball court. Then he used the money each year for things like painting the walls, putting up padding to prevent players from being injured and buying new uniforms. He also personally checked the equipment and made sure it was what they needed.

Everybody that worked with Ernie liked him. Most of the students liked him unless they were on the basketball team. The team didn't like all the Marine type of discipline he was giving them in practice, but they did like him. The one exception was a kid by the name of Gerry Farmer.

Coach Hoff had to teach a Driver's Education class, and part of that class met in the classroom. Coach Hoff was a pretty decent guy, but you didn't want to get him angry with you. Ernie was a talented, very strong wrestler, four letters in college, then wrestled and coached in the Marines. Well, one day Gerry Farmer was giving Ernie a rough time in class. He was a pretty big kid and he was challenging Ernie who to him seemed relatively small. He was sort of testing Ernie to see where his boundaries were. Coach Hoff decided he had about enough of Gerry's big mouth and he took him into the janitor's closet and hung him up on a hook. He was stuck there all period until the Coach came back after class and got him down. After that episode nobody ever gave Coach Hoff any trouble in any of his classes again.

In 1954 Gary tried out for the Varsity basketball team at Elm City High School. Again his performances in the tryouts were superior to any other guard they had on the team. When Gary checked the team rosters as soon as Coach Quinn posted them, he found his name on the JV list. Ronny Jay's name was on the Varsity list.

That season Gary's JV team won all of their games except two and went undefeated on their home floor. Their Varsity team was mediocre and won about half of their games. That season they had larger crowds at their home games than the Varsity did. People in the community of Elm City began to talk about how good the JV team was. Some even went so far as to wonder why Coach Quinn didn't use some of his JV team to help out the slumping Varsity team.

Gary was becoming popular around town. His mom went to all of his home games and his whole family sat around the radio listening to his away games if and when they were broadcast. A lot of people around town began to wonder why Gary who was an exceptionally talented athlete was not playing on the Varsity basketball team.

In 1955 Gary was sitting in study hall minding his own business quietly reading a book. Gary's study hall had approximately 200 students in it, and it was the largest classroom in his school. Elm City had 1,200 students, about 300 kids in each grade. Gary was reading at a table alone in the middle of the room near a window. Coach Quinn who normally didn't do anything that was irregular came storming into the study hall. "Pearn where are you?"

Gary raised his hand, "I'm right here Sir!"

Coach Quinn walked up to his table leaned over in his face, and in clear words that rang out through the whole study hall said, "You think you're going to try out for the Varsity tonight?"

"Yes Sir, I'll be there!" Gary said.

"Your hair is too long to be a basketball player on my team. Get it cut today before tryouts." Coach Quinn said.

"Yes Sir!" Gary said.

Coach Quinn turned around and stormed out of the room. Gary's face turned red with embarrassment. Gary always wore his hair in a neatly brushed flattop. He had a haircut just two weeks ago. The Elm City High School dress code said a boy's hair should not touch the ear, or the collar in back. Gary more than met those requirements.

Gary's barbershop was only two blocks from the school and the gymnasium where Gary had tryouts was two blocks from the barbershop. The Coach only allowed them ten minutes after school was out to be in the gym for roll call and they were expected to be dressed for tryouts by then. Gary thought if he ran as fast as he could to the barbershop, got his haircut, and then ran as fast as he could to the gym he just might get there in time.

Gary was excused from his last class five minutes early and he sprinted all the way to the barbershop. He was fortunate; when he arrived the barber sat in his chair reading a newspaper. When the barber saw Gary come in he got up and Gary sat down in the chair.

"Hurry up Floyd! I have Varsity tryouts in ten minutes." Gary said looking up at the clock on the wall.

"What do you want a quick buzz?" Floyd asked.

"Coach Quinn said I'd better have it done before tryouts today." Gary said.

"Why didn't you come in yesterday Gary?" Floyd said.

"The Coach told me today in study hall to get it cut." Gary said.

"He really didn't give you much time for it did he?" Floyd said.

"If I run I think I can make it." Gary said.

"Put your head down; I'll be done in a minute!" Floyd held Gary's head down until his chin touched his chest. He ran the humming clippers from the back of Gary's neck to the top on the back of Gary's head.

Gary was a neat, clean, handsome young man. His dark brown flattop was always brushed and he always wore clean clothes. His family was poor and he could not afford a lot of clothes. He always wore faded jeans and a white T-shirt to school. He only had two pairs of jeans so every night he washed the pair he wore that day by hand, and hung them up to dry, and he ironed the pair he had washed the night before to wear the next day to school. Gary's brilliantly blue eyes were always puppy-dog sad. He had dark bushy eyebrows that gave him a very distinguished look, and he always scrubbed his face until his skin was shiny. Gary's most memorable feature was a fantastic smile with perfectly white teeth, and then there was his unusual laugh that was uniquely his own.

Today was the beginning of Gary's junior season playing basketball and he felt good about making the team. He felt he was the best guard the Elm City Cougars had. He could feel the adrenaline flowing in his body as Floyd trimmed his hair.

"I think you're the best guard on the team." Floyd said.

"Thanks Floyd." Gary said.

"If you keep trying and don't give up you'll make it onto the Varsity team." Floyd said.

Floyd took the white pinstriped cloth off Gary and shook the hair onto the floor. He took a brush and brushed the hair off Gary's face and neck. Gary stood up reached into his pocket and pulled out the last two quarters he had.

"Here's four bits, thanks for the haircut!" Gary said.

"Good luck!" Floyd said.

Gary flashed that patented smile of his, that ear-to-ear grin and said, "See you in about three weeks."

Gary disappeared out the door like a mountain lion in pursuit of his prey. In the blink of an eye he was running down the street. Gary raced west on Morgan Street two blocks, headed toward the gym as fast as he could run.

Gary liked living in Elm City. He had a lot of friends and he could perpetually find a neighborhood game of basketball to play on an outdoor court. Gary also loved to swim and run, and he played golf when he could, earning the money to play by working occasionally as a caddy. He played baseball and football as well, but it was basketball he loved the most, and it was basketball that he played to his heart's content.

Gary had his heart set on playing Varsity basketball. He wanted to be the starting point guard for Elm City High School so badly that he could taste it. He knew basketball required a special kind of teamwork, more than just personal desire, basketball required an ability to know the other players and to be able to see them all at once all over the floor, and not only know where they were, but to intuitively know where they were going. The sport was like poetry to him.

For Gary basketball was fluid, perpetual and graceful motion. Gary had learned how to shoot a left-handed over the head jump shot because he was a southpaw. He would go straight up 38 inches into the air, pull his feet way up underneath him and release the ball with his fingertips. He extended his hand following through putting a beautiful arc and reverse spin on the ball. The basketball would actually make a loud swooshing sound as it ripped through the center of the net without touching the rim.

People around Elm City who had seen Gary playing on the Cougar's Junior Varsity thought he was the best point guard the team had ever had. Unfortunately, community popularity held little sway over Coach Quinn who didn't like Gary.

From Gary's freshman season Coach Quinn had recognized Gary's potentially great talent, he had seen his ball handling ability in every tryout, and he had made him play as a starting guard for the Junior Varsity team every year. Gary knew and had played one-on-one in his neighborhood with all the kids on the Varsity team, except for one, his nemesis, Ronny Jay. Ronny got away with having longer hair than any other guy on the team. He put a lot of grease in his hair and combed it back like a trucker.

Ronny was the one player that had what Gary believed should have been his position. Ronny was the starting point guard for the team. Gary felt he was a much better player than Ronny. Gary felt he was good enough to be a starter on the Varsity team. Gary always felt that Coach Quinn didn't give him a fair shake.

Sprinting two blocks to the gym was no problem for Gary who was in great shape, and soon he was inside the locker room putting on his canvas basketball shoes, and then he was down on the basketball court shooting baskets with the rest of the boys.

"PEARN, you're five minutes late!" Coach Quinn barked out across the entire gym with a twinge of meanness on his grave looking face.

"I'm sorry Sir, but you asked me to get a haircut." Gary said.

"That's no excuse for being late." Coach Quinn said.

"What if you were five minutes late for the Varsity bus for a tournament game?" Coach Quinn asked.

Gary shook his head, "I'd never be late."

"You've got that right because you're on JV again. You're never going to be on my Varsity team Pearn...." Coach Quinn said.

"Yes Sir!" Gary said.

Gary went back into the locker room, changed and came out of the gym with his head hung low. It was a long walk home going two blocks back up Morgan Street and across Elm City's town square. The park in the town square had hundreds of century old mature elm trees, and the emerald leaves of those large trees provided a canopy of shade for the entire park.

Gary had never before felt so disappointed as he did at that moment. Gary was disgusted with himself. At the center of Elm City's square was a Civil War Memorial Statue, and Gary sat down there to think through what had just happened to him. From his point of view at the Memorial he could see all the way out of town in four directions like the points on a compass. North and South Main Streets, and East and West State Streets joined at the square, and then went into a circular drive counter clockwise around the park's periphery.

Gary's biggest dream in life was to be the starting point guard on the Cougar's Varsity team. Right now his heart felt like it was breaking. He thought he didn't seem to have a chance. Everybody on that Varsity starting team seemed to have perfect lives. Their parents were happily married and they socialized with each other. Their father's held prominent business positions in the community.

Gary looked East, West, North and South. He looked at all of the hundreds and hundreds of boy's names on the monument who had given their lives in the Civil War. He read some of them out loud. He looked up at the top of the monument where Abraham Lincoln's words were carved in stone and read them aloud. He sat there for a long time thinking about Honest Abe's words.

Chapter 3

Elm trees in the square were grand and swayed majestically. American elms had broad green fuzzy leaves and thick black wrinkled bark. There were hundreds of elms all over the city. That's why they called it Elm City.

"Basketball is only a game." Gary said, as he began walking home from the square.

As Gary went home he began to realize it wasn't so bad. His dream was so close to becoming reality, but what could he do to make it happen? Gary decided that he would not only go ahead and start on the JV, but this would be his best season.

Yes Gary was poor and he didn't have a lot of things other people had, but he made the most of what he did have. He had a gift of a great ability to understand sports, a lighthearted sense of humor, and an outstanding amount of natural talent and athletic prowess. He had speed, and quickness with an ability to make you freeze with a look, give a head fake, and then drive around you on the court to make a play, while you wondered how he did it. Quite simply he was the kid that would beat you in any sport. He would find the way to win. He only had one problem in life. How was he going to become the star guard on the Cougar's Varsity basketball team when the Coach wouldn't let him tryout?

In 1955-56 Ernie Hoff coached a great basketball team. The Ashland Panthers Varsity team had finally found their stride and they were winning. The team Captain was Dick Edwards, a senior; he was their point guard. Then there were three juniors: Jack Lynn their tall center; Denny Bast their forward and their leading shooter; Jerry Conner a scrappy guy who played guard; and they had one sophomore on their starting team a tall forward Donny Field.

This team went undefeated on their home court, losing only four games all season. They lost a conference game to Petersburg on the road by four points. They lost an early tournament championship game to Elkhart by three points. They lost the last game of their season on the road at Easton, a conference team, by two points. Nine points was the total of points they lost by for the season. They were knocked out of the Chandlerville District Tournament that year by Easton, again in a tough hard fought game that was tied at the end. Easton won in the overtime at Chandlerville 66 to 60 bringing the total of points Ashland lost by for the year up to a total of 15 points.

Back in the middle of their season Jerry Conner set an unusual record that can never be broken. Jerry's unbeatable, untouchable record was set against the Virginia Redbirds in the biggest rivalry game of the year for Ashland. Virginia another small farm community was only ten miles away. Although, the game was being played at Virginia, most of the Ashland Panthers' fans had followed the team buses to the game and their fans were cheering louder than the Virginia Redbird's fans were cheering. The Panthers wore their purple uniforms with white trim and the Redbirds wore their white uniforms with red trim.

The Redbirds played a very tough defensive zone that was packed in tight against the Panthers. In a low scoring game at half time, neither team had made many baskets.

During half-time Coach Hoff said, "Jerry hold onto the ball until they come out of that zone!"

At the beginning of the second half, Jack Lynn, the Panthers' center tipped the ball to Dick Edwards who immediately passed it to Jerry. Jerry took the ball and began dribbling out near the center court line. Jerry who was an excellent ball handler dribbled with his knees crouched daring anybody to come out and guard him. The Redbirds stayed tautly in their zone. Jerry dribbled for the entire third period until the very last second, and then shot the ball. In 1955-56 there wasn't a shot clock, and unless the Redbirds came out of their zone, Jerry could dribble the whole period and it was legal. Nobody in the entire history of Ashland High School had ever dribbled the ball for a whole period. Jerry's record will never be broken because the rules have changed and the shot clock limits the amount of time a team may hold the ball without shooting.

Gary Pearn playing guard for the Elm City JV played a game against the Ashland Panthers Varsity team in December of 1955, here's how it happened. A few months earlier Coach Hoff had called Coach Quinn. Here's how their conversation went.

"We are trying to reinstate the Ashland Invitational Tournament this December and we'd like to invite your team." Coach Hoff said.

"I thought you guys gave up on that thing years ago." Coach Quinn said.

"After a lapse of six years this will be our twenty-eighth tournament, and we really need another team to fill out the bracket. Are you interested?" Coach Hoff asked.

"When is it?" Coach Quinn asked.

"It's the first Friday and Saturday of December. There will be two games here Friday night, and right after Saturday night's consolation game for third place, the winners will play for the Championship. There will be large trophies for first and second places and wooden plaques for third and fourth places." Coach Hoff said.

"Um....the Varsity has that date previously scheduled. Our JV team is undefeated this year and has been playing very good basketball. How would you feel about me sending the JV team?" Coach Quinn asked.

"Great, then I'll pencil in the Elm City Cougar's JV for the Ashland Invitational. Thank you Coach Quinn!" Coach Hoff said. And that was the end of their conversation.

The Cougar Varsity team truly didn't have any tournament games scheduled for December at all. The team had been playing so badly that they had lost their last six games in a row. Their best shooter Ronny Jay had pulled a hamstring and Coach Quinn had no idea when he would be able to play again. So to avoid the Varsity being embarassed by a loss to a tiny farm community team, Coach Quinn had offered up his JV team. Coach Quinn knew that the Ashland Panther's were having an exceptional season and he knew going in that Ashland would crush every team in the tournament. Coach Quinn was so twisted he actually wanted the JV to lose because they were having a better year than his Varsity, and he wanted nothing better than to see Gary Pearn's undefeated season end before Christmas.

That was how Gary got to play in the 1955-56 Ashland Invitational Tournament. In the opening round of the tourney, Ashland easily defeated Tallula. The Panthers had the lead early and steadily increased their lead throughout the whole game. In the second round Elm City's Junior Varsity defeated Balyki. Except for a brief time in the third period Elm City led throughout the whole game. Gary Pearn was their high scorer. In the consolation game Balyki defeated Tallula to capture third place honors. In the championship game the Panthers destroyed the Cougars JV team. At the end of the first period the score was 25 to 16. The Panthers were in command at half-time. In the second half they continued to build their lead and eventually defeated the Cougars JV by 35 points.

Gary had a couple of reasons to be happy that night. First and second place teams had their team photos taken for the front of the Sunday morning sports page in the Elm City Journal. Gary wearing his brightest grin sat in the center of the front row with the starting team holding the big Second Place Trophy for the 28th Ashland Invitational. In the second row of the photo in their warm-up suits were the second team and Coach Dan Norris. Their uniforms were crimson.

Gary chuckled to himself about what Coach Quinn might be thinking as he read the sports page over coffee the next morning. It was the first and the only trophy won by any Elm City team that season. Gary would be the point guard with the big smile holding the trophy.

Seated front and center for the Ashland team was Dick Edwards and he was holding the First Place Trophy. The whole Ashland team had big smiles on their faces. Even Coach Hoff who hardly ever was seen smiling had a little smile on his face. Those photos ran side-by-side on the front of the sports pages in both the "Elm City Journal" and the "Ashland Sentinel."

Gary's other reason for being happy was that for the first time since he was eleven he was seeing all of his old friends again. Gary was born in Ashland on January 10, 1939. He had gone to school in Ashland until the end of his fifth grade year when he had moved to Elm City.

It was a funny thing; the Echo, Ashland's yearbook published in May of 1956, inadvertently omitted the photo of the Panthers holding the trophy for winning their 28th Invitational Tournament. It was a strangely, weird and phenomenal omission. What they printed was the photo of Gary's Junior Varsity team with Gary holding the Second Place Trophy. Gary was actually the only player in the photo who really was a native of Ashland; he was the only person in the yearbook who was holding a basketball trophy. Gary's joyful countenance and the presence of that photo in the Echo was a premonition of what was to come in the future.

After the team photos Gary had a chance to say hello to his old friends who were crowding around him glad to see him after so many years. Jerry, Jack, Denny, and Wally were the same age as Gary and he had known them since first grade.

"Hello Gary," Jerry Conner said hugging his old best friend.

"Jerry you old son of a gun, how are you?" Gary said.

After Gary said hello to the rest of the guys Gary said, "Uncle Pete will let me use your gym on Sundays this summer why don't you guys come over and play some B ball with me?"

They all agreed to play on Sunday's in June. Gary's Uncle Pete Gutmann was Ashland High School's custodian. Now Gary's mom and Pete's wife were sisters and Gary's mom liked to go visit her little sister, Marguerite who she lovingly called "Snig," on Sunday afternoons. Whenever Gary came with his mom his Uncle Pete always unlocked the gymnasium door and gave Gary some basketballs because Uncle Pete knew just how much Gary loved to play basketball. In fact, everybody in Gary's family knew how much Gary loved basketball.

Gary was a good kid. Since his mom and dad had divorced Gary had tried very hard to take on the role of being the man around the house. He was very considerate and protective of his three sisters, and his little brother was very special to him. He always spoke lovingly of his little brother. While his little brother was growing up Gary was like a surrogate father to him. In return his little brother loved him and always looked up to him as a role model.

Gary's blistering speed and bulldog tenacity had gone virtually unnoticed by his old friends on the Ashland team during their championship game. Gary was fully aware that he was having a rare bad night, he seemed sluggish and he felt his timing was off, but he never gave up. Gary was surprised by the Panthers' ball playing abilities, they sure had Gary's focused attention and he was very impressed with the way they had handled the game and how well they played as a team. Except for that loss against Ashland on their home court Gary's JV team finished out their regular season undefeated.

Gary's sensational season went unheralded and unnoticed into the sports history record books. No matter what Gary thought about himself, Coach Hoff had noticed him when he played against the Panthers. What he alone had picked up on was Gary's passion for the game. He noticed that Gary was the spark that made that JV team go. He saw his beautiful 35 foot jump shot and he knew that without Gary's tough defensive effort Ashland would have outscored his team by sixty points. No matter how much Gary may have thought his efforts on the court that year went unnoticed, all of the basketball fans in Elm City loved Gary and he was very popular around town.

The summer of 1956 was the beginning of the end of Coach Quinn's reign of terror. It was that summer that the local writers for the Journal began to excoriate him in the sports pages for not moving Gary and some of the other great JV players up to help out the Varsity in the past season. Nobody in Elm City seemed to notice that what all those players had in common was they were from the wrong side of the tracks. Gary was painfully aware of Coach Quinn's unfairness.

All the seniors that played on the Elm City Varsity basketball team were graduating, and Gary's great JV team would become the Varsity team for next season. Ronny Jay would still be there though and Gary knew that even if Coach Quinn would let him play on the Varsity team he would sit on the bench all season watching Ronny who would be the starting point guard. That was the dilemma that was breaking his heart.

In 1956 the hot new girl's fashions were Poodle skirts worn with Bobbie socks, and black and white Saddle shoes. Elvis was a constant hit on the radio with songs such as "I've Been Searching," "Hound Dog," "Blue Suede Shoes," and "Love Me Tender." Frankie Lane and Doris Day had hit songs too, but nothing that summer topped the charts like Elvis. Every Sunday afternoon in June Gary Pearn could be found in the Ashland gym shooting baskets and playing with his old friends, Jerry, Jack, Dennis, Wally, they were all looking forward to their senior year. And a kid named Donny who was a junior that Gary was just getting to know played with them too. It was fun.

While Gary played basketball with his friends, the Ashland cheerleaders who were all friends with each other also drove to Elm City to go swimming. There were the Buker sisters Janet, a junior, and Barb, a senior, and then Bev and Sharon who were also juniors and Gloria who was a senior. While they were working on their tans they met and were pursued by three boys Eddy, John, and Ronny Jay. Gloria liked Ronny. Ronny drove a brand new '56 Ford that was turquoise and white with an all white interior because his dad Ronald Jay owned the dealership.

Jerry Conner worked part-time that summer as a soda jerk in the Ashland drug store. He and Denny rode around Ashland together in Denny's old jalopy that had a rumble seat. Denny's dad owned the town newspaper the "Ashland Sentinel." Denny's dad who was also the paper's editor asked them to be sports reporters and write all the articles about the basketball team and cover all the games as player reporters. Their mug shots and columns about the team and the coming season began to appear regularly in the weekly news. Denny was more interested in playing basketball and having fun than he was in writing so even though his picture was with Jerry's at the head of their column he let Jerry do most of the writing. Jerry had been inspired by a creative writing assignment the past year in school and found out how much he loved writing.

A couple of things happened in the hot summer that were about to make Gary's dream of being a starting point guard on a varsity team a reality, and Gary had no idea of what was about to happen. Gary's Uncle Pete had a brother named Frank who own a great restaurant in Ashland called Lillian's Knotty Pine Café. They had a majestic Seeburg jukebox and girls from school would sometimes go there to have a cherry, chocolate, or a vanilla, flavored pop and dance.

Donny Field, Jack Lynn, Denny Bast, and Jerry Conner were at the Café late one Saturday evening in August having hamburgers and talking about the coming season. They had high expectations for their coming year. The whole community had high expectations for them. They were the four starting players for the team and they had lost their senior Captain Dick Edwards because he had graduated. They really wanted to win their District tourney and maybe go as far as the State Finals in Champaign.

Jack and Denny had been named as All State Players on the starting team in Illinois after their magnificent 1955-56 season. They were being closely watched by college scouts. They all knew they had a great team they just were not certain about who could fill the guard position playing defense and running with their offensive fast break. They didn't have anybody in Ashland, they felt, that could give them what they needed, put them over the top, or fill the missing puzzle piece. What they desperately needed was a starting point guard that could help the team get past District, Regional, Sectional, and make it all the way to the State Finals.

"Too bad my friend Gary Pearn doesn't live in Ashland." Jerry Conner sort of half mumbled to himself.

"He's a great player." Jack said.

"Probably just what we need." Denny said.

"He's pretty fast and he's got a great jump shot." Donny said.

"Aw come on guys, I've always thought of Gary as my best friend, but really now—he's never played on a Varsity team. He doesn't have any experience." Jerry said cleaning his glasses with a paper napkin.

"I bet our DI—Coach Hoff can get him into shape." Denny said with a smile.

That was one point they all agreed on. So after talking it over, Jerry offered to go and talk to Pete Gutmann to see if he could help get Gary to come to Ashland to join their team.

One week later on Friday morning Jerry found Pete at the high school and talked with him about Gary.

"You know Jerry, Coach Hoff was talking with me earlier this morning, and he said he wasn't sure who he would be able to find to play point guard for the team." Pete said.

"Isn't that a coincidence? Last Saturday we sort of held a team meeting at the café and the guys decided to ask if you would have a talk with Gary about joining our team." Jerry said.

"Well, sure I'll ask him, but I don't know exactly what he'll say. If you come by the gym tomorrow before noon I'll let you know what he says." Pete said.

When Pete went home for lunch Marguerite had a hot homemade meal waiting for him.

"How was your morning dear?" Snig asked.

"Coach Hoff came and talked to me this morning." Pete said.

"He did?" Snig said.

"Yes I was outside smoking my pipe, and he said, 'When Dick Edwards graduated he left a big hole to fill.'" Pete said.

"The last time Dee was here she told me that Gary was brokenhearted because he's not going to get to play much this year in Elm City." Snig said.

"Then just before lunch Jerry Conner came by and he told me they had a team meeting and they all wondered if I would ask Gary to come and play ball this season at Ashland." Pete said.

"I think that's just a wonderful idea." Snig said.

"I was thinking I might go over to Elm City after work and see if Gary will come over for the weekend. If you don't mind, I want to go alone that way I can have a nice talk with him on the way back." Pete said.

"I'll have a good hot supper ready for you both when you get home. I just think it's a wonderful idea." Snig said.

"Gary will want to play ball in the gym Saturday morning so I'll talk with Coach Hoff and have him come to the gym early so I can introduce them. You know, I don't think Gary and the Coach have ever been introduced." Pete said, finishing his last bite of pie and lighting up his pipe.

Pete was a quiet character. His custodian job at the school was the only job he'd ever had. He was always there in the background quietly keeping the school in shape. He did an excellent job. All the students and the people in the community loved him.

Pete married Snig Weaver right out of high school and went to work as a custodian at the school and saved his money and built a cozy little house with his own hands just two blocks from the school. He loved to garden and grew the most delicious tomatoes that he always gave away to people.

He took care of a lot of the kids at school without any bravado. If someone needed a new pair of shoes, or a winter coat, they would suddenly appear. If someone didn't have lunch money Pete was the one that would stuff a few dollars into their pocket. Most of all Pete was a good listener. Everybody in the community knew him, liked him, and relied upon him, at one time or another everybody went to him for advice.

Pete didn't talk a whole lot, but when he did have a suggestion, and gave a piece of advice, it was always a comfort, always the exact solution for the given problem. After work that afternoon Pete was enjoying the sixteen mile drive through the countryside to Elm City.

Chapter 4

In 1956 on a sweltering hot humid August afternoon Gary Pearn felt exhausted. He was just walking home from football practice minding his own business. Gary played halfback on the Varsity football team. He was on the second team, but he didn't mind being a second string running back because the guy who was on the starting team was much bigger, much faster and an all round better halfback than he was. Besides, Gary got in the game almost as much as the first string halfback did, and they both had an impact on the game.

Gary had fun in Elm City. Everybody enjoyed his friendship because he had the ability to say the right thing at the right time. He could always make you laugh. He was always a clean well mannered kid. A lot of kids his own age respected him for his tough competitive attitude and his desire to win in sports. This was apparent to his teammates who played football with him on the Elm City high school team. In the huddle he was always humble and no matter what play had preceded, he might have had a 40 yard run, he was always ready to put it behind him and get on with the next play.

It was a swelteringly humid hot August day and Gary was walking home from football practice just minding his own business when a brand new 1956 Ford that was turquoise and white with a white interior pull up beside him and honked. Ronny Jay and his two pals Eddy, and John were in the car.

"Hey Pearn you want to have some fun?" Eddy said out the passenger window.

"Get in and we'll give you a lift home." Ronny said.

Gary had been in basketball practices with Ronny in the gym for the past three seasons and Gary hadn't had anymore trouble with him since that time in the locker room when Gary had broken his nose. Since that time Ronny had seemed totally insouciant. Gary was tired and he welcomed the thought of having a lift home. Gary got into the back seat beside John. They all seem innocuous and amiable enough.

John handed Gary a cold can of beer and Gary laughed as he opened the can and took a long drink. Everybody in the car was drinking. Ronny was driving too fast. He wasn't afraid of getting into trouble with the police because he knew that no matter what happened his dad would get him out of trouble. They broke the speed limit all the way up to the town square laughing and telling jokes. They circled the square about four times zigging and zagging around between cars and speeding when John said, "Hey let's go out to Nichol's Park."

Gary only lived a block from the square, but he decided to go around Nichol's Park and back with Ronny and his pals. John gave Gary another can of cold beer and Gary drank it. Nichol's park had a swimming pool, a golf course, a baseball field and three small lakes. They were all interconnected by one long curving asphalt road.

Ronny pulled his car in beside the grandstand at the ball park. From where they were, they could see part of one of the lakes and the empty baseball diamond. Nobody could see them because they were hidden from any outside view by the grandstands. They got out of the car and finished drinking their beer.

"Do you remember that day when you broke my nose?" Ronny asked crumpling a beer can and tossing it aside.

"You started it and I finished it." Gary said.

"Oh yeah, but I told you it wasn't over...." Ronny Said.

At just that moment Gary was punched in the right cheek so hard it knocked him backwards. He wasn't sure which one of the three boys had hit him. He shook it off just as he felt somebody kick him in the stomach. He pulled himself up and all four of the boys were engaged in one hellacious brawl. Gary knocked one boy's tooth out. He wasn't sure whose tooth it was, but he saw it go flying away. Two of them would have a black eye; he wasn't sure who they were either. It all happened so fast. Then just for a moment it seemed to him everything went black. He woke up just in time to see Ronny Jay driving away in his new car. He heard them all laughing as they pulled away.

Gary had fought valiantly even though he was physically exhausted from football practice long before Ronny and his pals showed up. Gary had the unmistakable taste of blood in his mouth when he sat up. It was a small cut at the corner of his lips. He smelled the stale scent of beer on his breath. He felt a painful bruise the size of a small grapefruit across his right cheek. He had welts and bruises on his stomach, back, and both arms and legs; and the worst thing of all to him was the fact that he had ripped his best pair of jeans and there were gaping holes in the knees. "At least they knew they were in a fight this time." Gary said brushing off the dust. He picked himself up and started walking. He was about a mile away from home. Other than those knocks and bruises he would have for the next couple of weeks Gary suffered no permanent injuries, nothing was broken or sprained. He was simply worn out. He laughed out loud at the thought of how bad he would look to his mom, sisters and little brother when he got home.

When he walked in his front door about twenty minutes later his Uncle Pete was there waiting for him and he greeted him with a smile.

Everybody noticed the bruises on his arms and face.

"Oh that," Gary laughed, "We had a pretty tough practice today!"

"Your Uncle wants to know if you'd like to go spend the weekend with him and Snig." Gary's mom said.

"Sure, I'd love to. Hey Uncle Pete can I go to the gym and shoot baskets tomorrow morning?" Gary asked.

"I think that would be a fine thing. I talked with Jerry Conner and he's going to come and play ball with you." Uncle Pete said.

"Wow that will be great. He's my best friend. I haven't seen him since June. Just let me get cleaned up a little." Gary said, and he went into the bathroom washed his face and hands, scrubbed his dirty neck. He wet his hair and put some gel in it that made his flattop stay standing straight up when he brushed it. He put on the only other pair of jeans he owned and a clean T-shirt. When he came out of the bathroom he looked like a different boy. He grabbed a small canvas bag and put his toothbrush, basketball clothes and shoes into it and zipped it up.

While Gary was in the bathroom loud enough that he could hear through the door Uncle Pete said, "Aunt Snig said she'd, 'have a good hot supper waiting for us when we get home.'"

Gary's mom was a waitress at the Elm City Café that was just off the square and she barely earned enough money to feed the six of them, let alone buy the clothing and school supplies they needed, and keep a roof over their head. That was why Pete had brought two large paper grocery bags full of fresh vegetables from his garden and gave them to her saying that they were from her sister Snig.

Gary's mom was a magnanimous person. She was a kind, patient, good hearted mom. She was always witty, cheerful and had a positive mental outlook. She had that rare and gracious quality in her personality of being able to laugh at herself. She could laugh at her own human imperfections. All of her family loved her for doing the best she could as their mother. She was smart too. She earned a perfect 4.0 GPA all the way through school. She graduated from Ashland High School at the tender age of 17 back in 1930. Her teachers loved her so much they excused her from her final exams because the only grade she ever got was an A. She possessed intelligence as well as magnanimity.

Incredibly Gary's mom, Dee Pearn always managed somehow to get to work six days a week and take care of her five children and provided for all of their needs. It was rough for them then though because they could barely afford the one bedroom flat they all shared. In it were their beds, one rocking chair and a gas stove. They didn't have any amenities, nor did they have a refrigerator, TV or telephone. They did however own a radio that plugged them into the current American culture. Sometimes they could even listen to games that Gary played.

Dee was very proud of Gary. She always felt so good about him whenever a regular customer at the Elm City Café came in for coffee and talked to her about his games. She tried to go to all of his games at home. She even went to some away games. When she couldn't go to an away game she would listen to his games on the radio when they were broadcasted locally.

Dee got up every morning at 4:30 A.M. and went to the Café. She had the door keys and opened the doors for early rising customers. They were closed on Sundays. She made coffee in a 50 gallon urn. She sliced all their homemade pies, filled the catsup and coffee cream containers and she turned on all the grills and ovens so they were ready when the cooks arrived. She was generous too. If a person was homeless, jobless, or just down on their luck and didn't have money to pay for a meal, Dee would quietly slip the check into her pocket and pay it out of her tips. If she didn't have enough money in tips to cover the bill, then she gave it to Mr. Sorrells the owner and Chef and he always took care of it no questions asked.

Dee was glad she had moved to Elm City. It troubled her that her son Gary was unhappy about not being able to play Varsity basketball. She felt he deserved a chance to play and wanted him to be able to do his best at a higher level just like Gary did. Gary was born in Ashland just like his three sisters Donna June, Phyllis Joanne, and Sara Jane. Gary was glad his little brother Victor was born in Elm City. That's me I'm the guy who's telling you this story. I was born just a few months after we moved to Elm City. Dee was born in the Texas Panhandle. Her mom and dad were Dustbowl farmers who gave up and moved to Illinois when she was seven. She started kindergarten at Ashland and she met her future husband Forrest Pearn in Kindergarten.

Gary liked living in Elm City where they had movie theaters. Gary loved going to movies. He loved seeing the latest horror movie and he loved films like "The Mummy," and "The Creature From the Black Lagoon." He loved Westerns like "On Top of Old Smoky" starring Gene Autry and Smiley Burnett. Smiley Burnett was his favorite movie star because Gary had his photograph taken with him when he came to Elm City to promote a new film.

Most of all what Gary loved about movies was the cartoons. Gary's favorite cartoon was Droopy. Droopy always made Gary laugh. As Gary's unique and boisterous laughter rang out across the theater any family member or friend of Gary's that might be there in the audience knew immediately that Gary was somewhere in the crowd.

Not only did Elm City have three movie theaters, they had a fantastic swimming pool, a golf course, a huge restaurant called the Ranch House that could serve 300 people and it had a drive-in, there also was a drive-in Movie Theater and several drive-in restaurants. Gary had 1,200 kids in his high school and he knew every one of them.

There was literally nothing for Gary to do in Ashland, except play basketball. Gary really didn't like Ashland because that's where his absentee dad lived. Gary once said, "When we lived in Ashland we were so poor when I was little; I remember we lived in a tiny white house that didn't have any furniture in it."

Gary also thought Ashland was a backward place. The main reason he thought that was a result of something that happened there when he was four-years-old. His little sister Sara Jane was born at home. Gary had been sitting on the front porch waiting for his sister to be born. When the Doctor who delivered her came out the front door Gary asked,

"How did my little sister get here?"

"I brought her in my little black bag." Doc replied.

Gary didn't believe him one bit.

Gary hugged his little brother and said goodbye to his mom and three sisters and followed Uncle Pete down the stairs and outside to where he was parked. He threw his bag in the back seat and they both got into the car. Uncle Pete was parked right in front of their door and he had to go up and around the town square to get back to Ashland. All the main businesses in Elm City were on the outside edge of the square and their entrances faced the park. All of the big department stores were located there.

"I saw in the paper that J.C. Penney's has a two for one sale on blue jeans. You wouldn't mind if we stopped over there and picked up some new jeans for both of us would you?" Pete asked.

"That would be great." Gary said.

While they were in the store shopping Uncle Pete said, "I want to introduce you to the Basketball Coach tomorrow morning. He's a young guy, only 27. He likes to shoot baskets and workout on Saturday mornings."

"He's a lot different than old Coach Quinn. I couldn't imagine him working out. Come to think of it....I've never seen him shoot a basketball." Gary said.

"Well I think you're going to like this Coach much better than him." Uncle Pete said.

"I bet I do." Gary said.

They both found two pairs of jeans that were their exact sizes and Uncle Pete paid for them at the cash register. They went out to the car that was parked on the square and got in. Pete started the car and drove around the square and went back past Gary's place and on out of town toward Ashland.

"Did you know that Dick Edwards graduated and that the Panthers need a Point Guard for their Varsity team?" Uncle Pete asked.

"ASHLAND NEEDS A POINT GUARD?" Gary repeated feeling a rush of adrenaline as the realization came upon him that this could be the solution to his biggest problem in life.

"They sure do need somebody talented to help them right now. They begin training next month." Uncle Pete said.

"I just can't believe it. It sounds too good to be true. You know I'm better friends with the kids in Ashland than I am with anybody at Elm City." Gary said smiling. Gary felt so happy about the possibility of playing Point Guard on a Varsity team. From this moment in time forward Gary's life would be forever changed for the better.

In Ashland Snig had made fried chicken, and when Gary and his Uncle Pete came in the kitchen door the aroma smelled so wonderful. Snig had mashed potatoes and chicken gravy and mouthwatering homemade biscuits, corn on the cob with melted butter, green beans, and tomatoes fresh from the garden. For dessert they had apple pie with a scoop of French vanilla ice-cream.

Swoosh; Gary buried a forty foot jump shot into the heart of the net, bright and early Saturday morning....

"That was a good shot." Coach Hoff said.

Morning light flooded the gym's old hardwood floor from every angle. It came in through the windows and through all the double doors that Pete had propped open. Coach Hoff caught the basketball as it dropped through the net and dribbled out to the top of the key, turned and shot a jump shot.

"Uncle Pete told me last night that you're looking for a guard to play on your team." Gary said, gathering in a rebound and making a lay up.

"We could sure use a player of your caliber Gary." Coach Hoff said.

"Did you know that I was born in Ashland?" Gary said.

"Really, that is amazing." Coach Hoff said.

"All the guys on your starting team are friends of mine; we went to school together until I was eleven." Gary said.

They began taking turns shooting free throws.

"I would love to try out for your team." Gary said.

"That's fine Gary, but I don't really have tryouts. I put the Varsity and JV through a rigorous conditioning program and I'm strict with discipline...." Coach Hoff said breaking into a genuine laugh. "The guys all think I'm a mean Marine DI. Everybody that makes it through the conditioning and follows my rules makes the team."

"I was impressed by the way you guys manhandled us in the Ashland tournament. Except for that one loss, my JV team over at Elm City would have been undefeated." Gary Said.

"We were undefeated on the home court last season. We came close to winning the District Championship. I know we could win it this year with you on the team. You'll have to officially transfer and that means you'll be required to sit out the first home game and the first away game." Coach Hoff said.

"I've always wanted to play point guard on a Varsity team. It will be a dream come true for me." Gary said.

"Show me what you've got, give me your best effort in practice and I'll put you into the game." Coach Hoff said.

Gary was flashing his big grin.

"I have to talk to mom about it tonight. My dad lives here and I can stay with him for my senior year." Gary said.

"Gary, I want you to know you can talk with me any time. If there is anything you need don't hesitate to ask me. If there is anything I can do to help you I will." Coach Hoff said.

"Thanks Coach. I want to do what I can to help the team. I'd like to go undefeated. I know Denny and Jack made the All State first team...." Gary said.

"Don't forget Jerry and Donny, they were mentioned for All State second team." Coach Hoff said.

"Wow, we have a really great chance then...we could go all the way in the State Championship Tournament. You know last season I had about three games that were my best games. In those games I was in a sweet spot where everything on the floor slowed down for me. It was like I was playing at full speed, but everyone around me was in slow motion. When that happened everything I did worked, I made every no look pass and I made every shot, it was fantastic." Gary said.

"Sounds like you were in a zone. I want to get you into such good shape that you will find that sweet spot in every game." Coach Hoff said.

"I fight hard. I never give up, but a couple of times last year while I was involved in the fight, fighting as hard as I could, everything became a dark shadow, and I lost consciousness." Gary said.

"Have you ever heard of Bill Russell?" Coach Hoff asked.

"The USA Olympics basketball player, yeah I've heard of him he's the greatest...." Gary said.

"When I was coaching the Marine Corps basketball team at Camp Pendleton he came and gave a talk to our team. I'll never forget one of the things he said, 'Every shadow has a bright light behind it. No matter how dark things look there is always a light behind every shadow.' Just keep looking for the light Gary." Coach Hoff said.

Jerry Conner came running across the gym floor.

"Hey Coach! Hi Gary how are you? How'd you get that big bruise on your face?" Jerry asked.

"Oh," Gary laughed, "That's nothing, I got it at football practice yesterday—I'll tell you all about it later." Gary said.

Coach Hoff threw the basketball to Gary.

"Take the ball out at center court. Jerry you guard him. Gary show me what you can do." Coach Hoff said.

Gary dribbled out to the center line with his right hand and turned around. He dribbled the ball in place three times, and then broke with blistering speed towards Jerry who was in front of him backing away. Gary drove straight at him, did a little head bobble fake left, then shifted the basketball into his left hand, and with bulldog tenacity accelerated to the right around Jerry as if Jerry's feet were stuck in molasses. With aplomb Gary leaped up without looking at the basket, extended his left arm out and up to the edge of the rim of the basket and the ball gently rolled off his finger tips through the cylinder into the net.

Coach Hoff caught the ball and walked over to Gary, he shook Gary's hand and said, "Welcome to Ashland Gary! I'll see you both of you guys at our first practice in a couple of weeks." And Coach Hoff gave Gary the basketball, and walked away, with his hand up in the air waving goodbye.

As the Coach disappeared through the tunnel, Gary jumped as high as he could and bounced the ball off the backboard, landed, and leaped again in perfect timing to push the ball up against the backboard. He did that little jumping drill five times in a row without stopping, all the time shouting with joy each time he leaped as high off the floor as he could.

Jerry Conner who had been standing there with his mouth wide open, in disbelief since Gary made his awesome move around him, said, "Congratulations Gary! I know you can really help our team."

"This is the happiest moment of my life. For three years I've been held back from playing Varsity ball. Coach Quinn never gave me a fair shake." Gary said, giving the ball to Jerry.

"You won't be a 'new kid' at school this year at all, just a wayward classmate that has returned, and

I'm really glad you're back. I can't wait to tell everybody you're going to be on our team. I'm going to write about you in my next article." Jerry said, shooting a jump shot.

"Thanks, I'm getting goose bumps just thinking about playing here for my senior year." Gary said.

Grinning, and tossing the ball to center court, Jerry said, "Just try and do that move on me again." In pure delight they challenged each other playing one-on-one for the next half hour until lunch, and then they walked over to Pete and Marguerite's house and they all ate lunch together. The first team practice, and sore muscles, were right around the corner. Gary's dream season was about to begin....

Chapter 5

Gary's Uncle Pete would go to all of Gary's games in the future. He was immensely proud to be Gary's Uncle. Like an inactive volcano, Pete was a calm and quiet man. On the inside though, he had molten lava; he had intense feelings of pride when Gary played basketball. Uncle Pete never told a soul that he had introduced Coach Hoff and Gary. That was the kind of great guy he was.

When Uncle Pete brought Gary back to Elm City he came upstairs and stayed for a visit while Gary excitedly told his mom everything that had happened. Gary was thrilled about being on the Ashland Varsity team, but he felt a little ambivalent about leaving his mom, sisters, and little brother. He had grown into the role of being the man of the house. It was a responsibility he did not take lightly. In the past summer Gary had worked for a local farmer putting up hay-bales all day long to help his family. It was hot, dirty, sweaty work, but it had made him stronger, and he had given all of his earnings to his mom.

"Gary I am so proud of you. I've always known you were an outstanding athlete and this is your opportunity to play basketball. It's your favorite sport. I think you should go to Ashland. Basketball is in your heart. If you didn't go you wouldn't be happy. I've always wanted you to be happy. Life is too short to be unhappy." Gary's mom said, and she put her hands on his shoulders and looked him squarely in the eyes.

"Be diligent and apply yourself, and you will go a long way." Gary's mom said.

"Gary is welcome to stay with us until he moves in with his dad." Pete said.

Gary packed a few things he had and hugged everyone and told them goodbye. He picked his little brother up and held him way up, high over his head, which made his brother laugh joyfully, and said, "I'll come back when I can and see you on the weekends."

And that's how my brother Gary left home to play basketball in the sleepy little farm community of Ashland....

There wasn't a whole lot of the stuff of which dreams are made in tiny Ashland, Illinois way back in 1956. But there was basketball. In September 1945, one month after WWII ended, Ashland Grade School's small first grade class included Dennis Bast, Jack Lynn, Gary Pearn, and Jerry Conner, four of the five who took the floor as starters twelve years later when the Ashland Panthers began their incredibly sensational senior season. Don Field, the other starter wasn't to start school until a year later in 1946.

Basketball was always there. It was basketball that brought everyone together in Ashland and provided the social life for the entire community during the 1956-1957 season. And ultimately, it was basketball that had kept the kids playing together for hours on end

on the out-doors court at the old grade school during chilly, even cold recesses before and after school. Oh, the hours they spent playing basketball on that playground, or at the old basket behind the Christian Church, and occasionally when Pete Gutmann would let them in the high school gym, usually with no adults present, just a bunch of kids dreaming of greater days ahead. It was evident early that they all saw that being on the high school basketball Varsity team was as fine a goal as anybody could have in Ashland. And of course, it was that goal that brought Gary back for senior year.

In mid-September Gary sat on the gym bleachers dressed out for his first practice along with 21 other kids. Coach Hoff came in dressed in sweats and said, "Welcome to practice. We have a new teammate joining us this year Gary Pearn." The other kids clapped and cheered. Gary's reputation had preceded him.

"After a couple of games Gary will be replacing Dick Edwards in his leadership position as our starting point guard. I expect a lot from the team this year. This is without a doubt the best team Ashland has ever started. You young men are as good as any other ball players in Illinois. I expect to win District and go well beyond that this year.

Now is the time....begin to strive for perfection, and for perfect conditioning that will prepare you to reach perfection. You must reach perfection. Be superior, be dominant, and be competitive at the highest level. We are not going to play anybody this year; they have to play us. We will never give up in a game. We begin today by shaping up, working on a positive mental attitude and by getting into better physical condition than any opponent we will face. For the next two weeks we practice with NO BASKETBALLS, calisthenics and running will be our main focus for the next 10 practices. I'm going to demand discipline and a 110% effort from you at all times. I won't be however, asking you to do anything I won't do myself. Follow me men! This is the GRINDER!" Coach Hoff said, running up the wooden bleachers in a mad dash with both the Varsity and JV players chasing him.

The bleachers were high and Coach Hoff ran every tiny little step up and down across the gym, down the side of the tunnel, crossed in front of the tunnel and went back up to the top of the bleachers. And then he ran across the top of the bleachers, back down every tiny little step and then ran across the gym. Then Coach Hoff ran all the way around the floor and looped back to the spot where he had originally started his mad dash up the bleachers. Over his shoulder he yelled, "Follow me men! Stay behind me and pace yourselves. Never lead unless you know where you are going." That was the completion of one lap. They ran 40 laps. Everyday to begin warming up they ran 40 laps on the GRINDER.

"Now spread out and find your own permanent spot on the bleachers. Ok, now we begin to separate the men from the boys doing 50 jumping jacks, followed by 100 sit-ups and 100 push-ups." Then Coach Hoff took them onto the floor and demonstrated the Grasshopper. Drill Instructors in USMC boot camp called this exercise bend-and-thrusts, the recruits however, had a more literal sobriquet for the exercise by adding a few expletives. Coach Hoff called them Grasshoppers because he added a flourish at the end that made the exercise unique.

In the Grasshopper the Marines had an exercise designed to tear down every known muscle in the human body. It went like this. First bend over and touch your toes, then put your hands down flat, then bend your knees and kick your legs back into a pushup position. Next do a push up. Then reverse the motion bringing your legs back up and stand up, then throw your arms up as high as you can and leap up as high as you can. That was one Grasshopper. It was done as he counted to eight. Everyday they would do 100 Grasshoppers.

By now guys were moaning and groaning. Imagine farm kids that had worked in the spring and summer from dawn to dusk, who were healthy, strong and robust to begin with complaining about a few exercises. It made Gary laugh. When Gary laughed it made Jerry Conner who was right beside him bust out in uncontrollable laughter and soon all the kids in the whole gym would be laughing.

"This coach is great." Gary said to Jerry, "He's making me use muscles I didn't even know I had."

Then Coach Hoff began to scream in his meanest Marine Corps voice, "NO PAIN, NO GAIN! MEN HOW DO YOU KNOW YOU'RE ALIVE? WHEN YOU CAN'T FEEL ANY PAIN---THEN YOU'RE DEAD! Now work it."

He made them do leg lifts until they felt like their legs were made of steel. They had to do 25 reps of leg lifts that began by lifting their legs and then dropping their legs, six inches, four times, until they were back on the floor. If anybody couldn't hold their legs up then Coach Hoff put his foot on their chests and made them struggle until they had it right.

By the end of the first day of practice Gary thought he was going to die. After working in the hay fields all summer and recently finishing six weeks of football practices at Elm City, Gary thought he was in pretty good shape to begin with.

After the calisthenics and all the moaning and groaning ended Coach Hoff made them run endless sprint drills across the basketball court and back for an entire hour. In those dead heat all out sprints Gary was out front and he came in first most of the time, but after a while it all seemed a blur....

After the running drills everybody was soaking wet with sweat except Glenn Savage. Glenn had a rare medical condition that prevented him from sweating very much at all.

Before Coach Hoff sent them away for showers he said, "One of my goals this year is to see if I can make Glenn break a sweat." And that made the team laugh.

"No smoking or drinking! If I catch you, you're off the team. No chocolate, no chocolate milk or milkshakes; I'd rather see you drinking a bottle of beer than a bottle of pop." This also drew laughter from the team. "Get to bed early every night because the only sleep that counts is the sleep you get before midnight. Ok, line up and get your vitamin."

At the end of every practice Coach Hoff gave them huge yellow multivitamins that looked as big as a horse pill, and he expected them to go into the shower room and take the pill. For the entire school year you could find vitamin pills floating in the lavatories in the school restrooms.

As he was passing out the vitamin pills he said, "Have a good supper when you get home. Eat lots of vegetables and meat; go easy on the bread, potatoes and cake. Stay away from sweets. Do your homework, and I'll see you tomorrow, same time, same place."

Although Gary hadn't fully realized it, the guys on the team knew that Coach Hoff's basketball practices were tantamount to going through Marine Corps boot camp.

Gary had moved in with his dad. So after showering and dressing Jerry Conner and Gary walked home. Jerry lived half way across town and went right by where Gary lived.

"Hey thanks for writing about me in your article in last Friday's paper." Gary said.

"I'm glad you liked it." Jerry said.

"Yeah it made me laugh especially that part about how your muscles get sore from basketball practice." Gary said.

"You might not be sore now, but just wait until tomorrow morning....and we've got these workouts every day after school for the next two weeks." Jerry said.

"Your muscles might get sore, but mine won't." Gary said, and he held up his arms, began wiggling his biceps, and breaking into his contagious riotous laugh. Whenever Jerry heard Gary laugh it always made him laugh too.

Jerry Conner and Gary Pearn were the best of friends and they played their guard positions so well together that they were like bookends. Jerry was more muscular and weighed about forty more pounds than Gary. Being a little lighter made Gary a step quicker. Jerry was fiercely proud of being a guard on the Panther's Varsity. This would be his third year starting in that position so he had more experience than Gary. Jerry thought Gary had a great sense of humor and a sharp cutting wit. They loved to have fun together and hatch up pranks to play on people they were close to, and in a small school like Ashland that meant everybody. With Gary's arrival at AHS, counting the boys and the girls too, they now had 19 students enrolled as seniors for the graduating class of 1957.

One thing that Gary, Jerry Conner and Jack Lynn all had in common was they were all from undeniably poor families. They were lucky to be playing in Ashland that year. If they had been playing for Elm City, Coach Quinn would have made them sit on the bench all season, if he had even let them on the team at all. Coach Quinn really had a problem; anybody that he considered to "have penury problems," or if they came from what he called, "a broken family," then he never would treat them as equal to the other kids, or give them a fair chance.

Coach Hoff was a man with a different perspective. He knew that it wasn't a kid's background that held him back. For Coach Hoff it was all in the kid's mental attitude and conditioning. If you threw in a little talent, speed and natural ability then you might really have a team. Considering the friendship and chemistry of his current Varsity ball team Coach Hoff was more than a little excited about his team. In order to save on expenses Coach Hoff and Superintendent Bierman shared a two bedroom house. When Coach Hoff went home after the first night of practice he was so excited he told Mr. Bierman that this could be the best team Ashland ever had, and he thought they not only had a real chance at winning their District, but they could go on as far a the Sweet Sixteen, and if they were lucky make it into the State Championships over at the University of Illinois gymnasium in Champaign, Illinois. That wonderful news excited the Superintendent and the next day he told someone he had lunch with, and with Ashland being a very tiny town, you can guess what happened next, before long everybody in town had heard what the Coach had told Mr. Bierman.

For Gary the practices with Coach Hoff were the same routine every day for the first week, and he became just as sore as the other players. But he would never give up. Being that sore actually felt good to him. He liked being able to feel muscles in places he didn't know he had them.

Also, in mid-September Ashland High School held their tryouts for Cheerleaders. The entire student body of around 100 students assembled in the gym and sat on the bleachers. Each young woman who was trying out had to come out in front of the crowd and lead them in a cheer. After each of the girls had led one cheer, the students would then vote for their top five choices, and those five girls who received the most votes would be the Varsity Cheerleaders for the class of 1957. They repeated the same process for their Junior Varsity Cheerleaders.

Then at the beginning of the second week of practices Coach Hoff brought a four-by-six foot poster in and taped it against the wall in their locker room. He told the team that they would keep a daily log on the poster. Every player would be required to find the line with his name and enter how many free throw shots he hit each day. They had to shoot at least 100 free throw shots every day, but not during their regularly scheduled practices. During school days they were allowed to leave any class of their choice for 30 minutes with a pass to go to the gym, which was located in the school, and shoot baskets.

Usually they did that in pairs. Jerry and Gary frequently took their free throw time together, and Jack and Denny did the same, but not always. Sometimes each of them shot with Donny. And sometimes they shot their baskets with Wally Wheeler, or with any of the other four boys who were on the second team in the Varsity. A lot of times though Donny Field shot his free throw baskets with Coach Hoff.

By this point in time everybody in town had heard the good news about the quality of the Ashland team that was about to take the floor in a couple of weeks for their first game. Jerry Conner wrote a column on how good they felt their team could be; it was all about how they not only wanted to repeat this year going undefeated on their home court, but fully expected to extend it to the away games and have an undefeated season. He reiterated that he thought Gary Pearn could really help their team because every day in practice Gary became more impressive and his confidence level was growing.

It was also about this time that people around town were trying to guess who Coach Hoff might use to replace Dick Edwards, the guard who had recently graduated from the starting line-up. Speculation on that topic was running high. Although, Coach Hoff and the team pretty much knew Gary would be the point guard that made the five man starting line-up, they weren't telling anybody. People would just have to find out at game time on the day Gary was first allowed in the game.

In one of Jerry's articles Mr. Bierman was quoted saying, "This ought to be our year to win, since most of the boys have experience, and two winning seasons behind them. This should be the year they go all the way."

Then, Charles Forman the local Auctioneer who served as the official home-game scorekeeper was quoted saying, "I think we have the best bunch of boys and team we've had in ten years. They should go undefeated and go to the State Tournament."

Coach Hoff was quoted saying, "Barring injuries and sickness, Ashland could enjoy one of its finest seasons."

And the rest of his article said the following: "Basketball fans will be treated to a new look at the first home game. The gym is getting a new coat of paint. Pete Gutmann and Elmer Woods have been working on it with the help of the basketball managers Bob McCarthy and Jim Wright. Come out to the games and see the improvement."

Sports writers at the State Capital in Springfield had articles covering the Ashland Panthers as well. One sports writer went so far as to say he thought, "With senior forward Dennis Bast, and their center Jack Lynn, the Ashland Panthers have the best 1-2 punch in the state. Both are talented young men that the university and college scouts are watching closely." Little did they know that waiting in the wings the Panther's had their secret weapon Gary Pearn, whose talent at point guard had been kept hidden by Coach Quinn in Elm City and was only beginning to bloom. Right now there were three pretty important people in Gary's life that believed in his talents: his mom, his Uncle Pete, and his new Coach Ernie Hoff.

But the Panthers were anxious for his unveiling. Gary's remarkable talent was about to raise the level of Panthers' basketball team, lifting it higher than ever before. The Panthers were almost ready to display their 1957 model team; a flawless full-court zone defense powered by their fast breaking run-and-gun offense. Gary was like that proverbial thoroughbred that had been "run hard and put away wet" when he had played ball on the Elm City Junior Varsity. With the proper care, conditioning and nurturing, Gary had unlimited potential that was about to surface and become fully realized. Nobody yet knew just how great a player Gary Pearn was about to become, not even Gary.

Chapter 6

As a team the Ashland Panthers had a striking look. They came on their home floor in an intimidating fashion running as fast as they could in a line circling the court and coming back to their basket for warm up drills. They did it with machine like military perfection, and they drew the full attention of the cheering home crowd as well as the opposing team. At home the Panthers wore white uniforms with purple lettering. Each Panther wore white knee length socks with a wide purple stripe at the top and white knee pads and they wore high-top white canvas Converse All Star shoes with purple laces.

The opponent in their first game of the season was Tallula; the same team they had beaten last year in their first game of the Ashland Tourney. Jerry Conner's game report in the "Ashland Sentinel" said, "Tallula took a 2-0 lead, then Don Field made free throws to tie it up. The only bright spot in the game was the effectiveness of the Panthers' zone press. After that Ashland led all the way. Panthers' shot 34% from the field, but missed only four free throws. Tallula's smaller more aggressive boys gathered in most of the rebounds as the Panthers played a very ragged and poor brand of ball. Jerry Conner was the high scorer of the game with six field goals and three free throws for 15 points."

Gary Pearn had sat in the crowd watching the game as Jerry, Jack, Denny, and Donny accompanied by Glenn Savage took the floor at the start of the game. In the middle of the fourth period Edgar Birch replaced Donny Field. The game was a sleeper and they were just going through the motions for the win.

There is no way Tallula could have won that game against the Panthers in a million years.

During the second game of the season Gary stayed at home with his dad and wrote a paper for his English class. He listened to the second half of the game on the radio with his dad. The Panthers traveled to Greenview for their first conference game of the season. Their road uniforms were deep purple with white lettering. Greenview had lost their first game to Balyki, so they were going all out for a victory. Greenview held the lead during the entire first half.

Coach Hoff played the same five Panthers for the whole game; Jerry, Jack, Denny, Donny, and Glenn Savage. As Gary and his dad listened to the second half, the game was a hard drawn battle, a real nail biter. This game went down to wire. Greenview had a team that was intensely stubborn and fought to the end. However, in the second half Ashland came from behind and had a two point lead with ten seconds left to go in the game. McGee made a lay-up for Greenview to send the game into overtime. Denny Bast and Donny Field, Ashland's two forwards scored in the overtime, but near the final seconds the Panther's led by only one point. Miller for Greenview had a chance for the victory at the close of the game when the referee gave him a one-and-one free throw, but Miller missed the first one, ending the game.

Gary's dad, Forrest Pearn turned off the radio and said, "Sounded like they could have used you in the game tonight. I hope you will be able to help them win."

"Thanks dad, I plan too..." Gary said.

Gary full of nervous energy sat on the bench watching the Panthers' third game. At half time he had been unimpressed by the way the Panthers were playing. The Panthers looked sluggish from the bench. In this game against Pleasant Plains Coach Hoff had started Wally Wheeler along with Jerry, Jack, Denny and Donny, but Pleasant Plains was pounding the boards and making Ashland look bad. By the end of the third period the Panthers led by only three points. At that moment Coach Hoff said, "15, you're going in the game." Gary went to the scorekeeper's table and let them know he was going in at the beginning of the fourth period.

It was magical for him. His long desired dream was coming true. He was going into his first Varsity game. The effect it had on his body was that a tingling flash ran from the top of his head to the bottom of his spine. His nervous energy dissipated as he walked out onto the floor.

Everything seemed to be going in slow motion for him from the moment Jerry tossed the ball in to him. Gary grinned at the kid from Pleasant Plains that was trying to guard him. Dribbling with his left hand he exploded around his opponent and outran him up the floor. Then without looking he passed the ball immediately towards Denny. Jumping high for the ball, Denny caught it turning in the air, and released a fading jumper as he was going down, and swoosh, the ball hit nothing but net.

The Panthers had a five point lead. As the kid who was just trying to guard Gary came dribbling toward him with the basketball, Gary smiled as he swooped the ball away with his left hand, dribbled once, then threw a baseball pass to Jerry. Jerry Conner had known that Gary was about to get his first steal in the game and had immediately started running full steam toward the basket. Jerry and the ball arrived at the free throw line at the same instance and

Jerry caught it in stride dribbled once and executed one of the finest right handed finger-roll lay-ups he had ever made, and as smooth as that, Ashland had punched the lead up to seven points and they never looked back. Jerry had been alone. All the other players were still in the backcourt. That was the jump-start of the Panthers lightning like, fast-break offence that would electrify crowds all season long.

Lightning struck twice because a few seconds later Gary stripped the ball again and Jerry got another lay-up. Then a fluke happened when Pleasant Plains sent a new kid into the game from the bench and he was confused, and shot at the wrong basket, and scored two more points for Ashland. The score had jumped to an eleven point lead 50 to 39 in the first two minutes of the fourth period with Gary on the floor. From that point on the entire Panther team turned on the steam scoring 16 more points and the final score was Ashland 66, Pleasant Plains 51. Denny was the high scorer for the night with 26 points, and with three victories under their belt, the Ashland Panthers were beginning to roll.

Waverly, Illinois was the host for Ashland's fourth game of the season. The starters for the game were Jerry, Jack, Denny, Donny, and Wally Wheeler. After the first three minutes they were leading by ten points and Waverly called for a time-out. Coach Hoff then put Gary in for Jerry, Glenn Savage in for Wally, and Jim Ratliff in for Donny. Coach Hoff told them to keep the full court zone pressure on and get the fast-break going. After two more minutes Coach Hoff put Donny back into the game in place of Jim Ratliff and Jerry back in place of Glenn Savage.

Jerry and Gary were playing guard, Denny and Donny were playing forward, and Jack was their dependable center. Coach Hoff had found the combination that would become their starting five. With this group of players in the game they looked invincible to opposing teams. Their defense was impenetrable, dense and impassable. Their offense was lightning quick with five excellent shooters.

Magically their tough zone began feeding their fast-break and they jumped out to a thirty-five point lead over the Waverly Scotties. A freak accidental shot occurred when Denny grabbed a defensive rebound and tried throwing a baseball pass all the way down court to their center Jack who had led the other Panthers on the fast-break. Denny's pass flew entirely over Jack's head into the basket. It was the most amazing shot of their entire 1957 season. From that play on, Waverly lost the wind from their sails. Denny was the leading scorer that night with 18 points.

On the bus ride home Gary told Denny, "That was the most amazing play I've ever seen. I will never forget watching your full court pass sail into the hoop as long as I live."

So far that was the best they had played all season long. The whole team played with fire in their belly. They began creating new plays in midstream as they ran full speed ahead. It became a game of high voltage perpetual motion for them. It was fun.

Jerry Conner did everything he could to help Gary make a smooth transition as a starter on the Panthers Varsity team. Jerry could remember his own pre-game nerves giving him fits the first season he had started as a Varsity ball player and he did everything he could to sooth Gary's nerves before each game.

Gary was quite nervous in his first game getting the starting nod. Gary's first start came in the fifth game of the season, at home. They were playing the Petersburg Blue jays. This was an important test for Ashland because the Blue jays were one of the three teams that had beaten them last season. Jerry had tried his best to keep Gary laughing before the game to try and relieve his nervous tension. But Gary was still nervous. After a couple of minutes in the game though Gary forgot about his nervousness when the Panthers offense began to roll and they defeated the Blue jays 84 to 63. That night Denny was hot on the home court and Gary kept feeding him the ball. Denny finished the game with 33 points. The Panthers scored 16 free throws that night. Gary was gaining more confidence with every game and in his first game starting in Dick Edwards' old point guard position he had contributed nine points.

Ashland could be such a bore with nothing to do. Most of the people at AHS walked everywhere they wanted to go in town. That autumn the Varsity Cheerleaders that had been democratically elected by the students were Gloria and Barb who were both seniors and Sharon, Bev and Janet who were all juniors. Sharon was one of the luckiest girls in school because her generous parents let her drive their black Ford truck, and occasionally they would let her use their brand new car, also a Ford, so she could take the other cheerleaders over to Elm City, or Springfield to see a movie, or eat, or go roller skating. In the summer time they went to Elm City to swim at the Olympic sized outdoor pool at Nichol's Park.

It was a lazy Saturday afternoon when Sharon gathered the other cheerleaders into her mom and dad's new white Ford and they were driving around in Ashland looking for anything to do to have fun. Most of the basketball games where they cheered for their Panthers were usually held on Tuesday and Friday. Saturday nights were a constant bore. They were out looking for fun when they decided to go to Springfield and see a movie.

Earlier that night Barb called Gloria to ask her what shoes she was going to wear. Gloria said, "Let's wear our black and white saddle shoes tonight." Then they called the other girls to let them know what shoes to wear. Janet called Sharon to find out which skirt she was wearing, and they all decided to wear their newest poodle skirts. So the girls would all be wearing sweaters with little white collars, poodle skirts, and saddle shoes with their white Bobbie-socks rolled down.

They drove out of Ashland headed towards Springfield. When they got to Springfield they couldn't find a movie that any one of them wanted to see so they cruised the loop between two drive-in burger joints. It was the loop all the kids from all over central Illinois cruised for fun. After cruising the loop twice, shouting at every guy in a hot car that they saw, they left the loop and drove out to Moonlight Gardens Roller Skating Rink and went roller skating.

They always had fun when they went skating together. The rink had a spinning ball made of tiny mirrors that reflected little bits of colorful light all across the rink. None of the cheerleaders smoked or did anything that would make their school look bad. They really enjoyed having fun.

The Panthers won their sixth game on Tuesday night at Bluffs. Jerry's Sport's article said, "The Panthers took an early lead and looked ragged in the first half, but still maintained an 11 point lead at half time. The Panthers slowed their game in the second half and took more deliberate shots that increased their shooting percentage. The final score was Ashland 76, Bluffs 58. Denny scored 26 points."

In their seventh game Denny Bast broke the Ashland school record for the most points ever scored by a player when he scored 38 points. Gary and Jerry knew Denny was making everything that night so they kept passing the ball to him every chance they had. They were playing at St. James where they used their full court zone press effectively in the first half to build a sixteen point lead at half time.

Here's how the Ashland Panthers' full court zone press defense worked. Gary would take his position at the center of the court, right where they had to jump up and tip the ball at the start of every game. Then Jerry would be up right by the guy on the St. James team who would be tossing the ball inbounds. Denny and Donny the two forwards would be even with the free throw line, but spread out to the sidelines with Donny on the right side and Denny on the left. So in the half court where the opposing team only had ten seconds to bring the ball across the center court line the Panthers formed an open diamond shape. Jack always stood on the free throw line behind Gary forming a 1-2-1-1 full court zone defense. Jerry would guard the man with the ball. Denny or Donny would then come up for a double team. This forced the ball handler to stop his dribble so they could steal the ball, or forced him to throw a bad pass. If the ball was passed, two other Panthers were there to intercept it and make a lay-up. If they didn't cross the center line in ten seconds then they turned the ball over and Ashland would get to bring the ball in at center court.

The Panthers' zone press defense rattled a lot of players and could annihilate a team. Most teams put their own zone defense into that half of the court underneath the basket they were defending. Coach Hoff also dropped back into a 2-3, or a 2-1-2 tightly packed zone after the Panthers had established a formidable lead. But that active full court zone press demoralized opponents and literally crushed their team spirit when they began to realize that they couldn't even bring the ball across their own center court line.

When the Panthers were in their full court zone press Jerry would be guarding the opponent, and then Donny or Denny would join him in the double team. That usually left Gary free to intercept a bad pass when the man being double teamed panicked. Gary made a lot of lay-ups that way and he also made a lot of assists because when Jerry, Denny and Donny saw that Gary had the ball they would break towards the basket. The first one there would receive a fast pass from Gary for an easily unguarded two point play. Then St. James would get the ball out, and the Panthers would apply the pressure of the full court zone again.

Ashland sometimes made ten or fifteen baskets in a row using this defense. One of the reasons it was so effective was that in 1957 most teams simply played a half court defense all the time. Opponents Coaches didn't know how to approach and break that type of pressure. Usually, in an average game a team could just walk, dribble and pass the ball back and forth between their two guards and bring the ball up across the center line without anybody ever guarding them at all.

The Panthers could shake a team out of their game plan in a couple of minutes by upsetting their offensive rhythm and destroying their ball handling confidence. St. James was one of those teams that couldn't take the Panthers' defensive pressure. The final score was Ashland 91 and the St. James Tradesmen 45. Not only did Denny set the school record with 38 points, but the Panthers had doubled the score on St. James. That night Ashland was only fouled five times by the Tradesmen, but Ashland made all of their free throws shooting 100% at the line.

The first Tournament for the 1957 Panthers was at Astoria. According to Jerry's sports column, "An extra bus will be provided for the Astoria Tournament by The Lettermen's Club. Anybody wishing to catch a ride could contact Janet Buker or Lynell Field." That meant for the tourney there would be three buses going to every game. The first bus was the team bus that carried the Coach, manager and players. The second bus was for cheerleaders and students from AHS. The third bus was for parents, fans, or anybody that wanted a ride to see the Panthers play basketball.

The Panthers also had an avid group of fans that drove their own cars to all the away games. That group of fans included The Conner's, Field's, Forman's, Buker's, Plattner's, Savage's, and Aggertt's families. Coach Hoff always tried to keep the players separated from the cheerleaders to keep the team focused on the coming game. He had a "No Talking" rule for the guys on the bus going with him to a game. He wanted them to save their energy. Everybody on the team obeyed the "No Talking" rule because Coach Hoff was like a stern father wearing his game face when they were on the bus. They maintained silence because they didn't want to get reminded by him on the bus about his silence rule. It was embarrassing to be the one caught talking and be the guy who made the Coach remind the team to focus on the business that was the main purpose of their road trip. Every player was responsible for wearing a coat and tie and for bringing their own uniform. The penalty for not having your entire uniform with you was you couldn't get dressed for the game, and you would not get to play.

Pete Gutmann always greeted and shook hands with every ball player as they boarded the bus in the school parking lot. He knew who the kids with poor families were and he did what he could to help them. He always wanted to be certain that Gary could afford a good meal if the bus stopped at a restaurant on the way home after a game and they always did. Gary's Uncle Pete would meet him at the bus and stuff a few dollars into his pocket as he got on the bus. It was always more than enough for Gary to pay for his own meal and he had enough left over to cover for a couple of his friends as well. Pete always stuffed money into his pocket secretly though and Gary was the only person that ever knew Pete was generously helping him.

The Cheerleaders bus didn't have a "No Talking" rule and they were much more fun to ride to the games with. Everyone going to the tourney felt like winners because Ashland was undefeated going into the tournament. The cheerleaders would cheer and sing all the way to the game. It was a social event for everybody on their bus.

This was the first time Ashland had ever entered the Astoria Tournament. Coach Hoff had entered the Panthers this season because he wanted them to play games that would provide more competition. One of the things he knew about his Ashland Panthers was that when the competition grew tougher the Panthers played their best ball.

In the first game Ashland was going to play a school called V.I.T., which was a school formed by joining three small farm communities: Vermont, Ipava, and Table Grove. These communities were much smaller than Ashland, but when combined into one high school their school was more than twice Ashland's size. In the first three periods it was nip and tuck all the way with V.I.T., but in the fourth period the Panthers superior conditioning became evident as they continued to run and gun tirelessly. Donny Field was playing the best basketball he had ever played at the Varsity level. Donny seemed to be in the right spot at the right time all night long. He seemed to be everywhere in the game. He grabbed most of the rebounds at both ends of the court, and he was the high scorer of the game with 21 points. Donny Field was the MVP of the game. Ashland had won their eighth straight game 50 to 47 and eliminated V.I.T. from the tourney.

Chapter 7

The next Panthers' game in the Astoria Tournament was with Illinois School for the Deaf (I.S.D.), from Elm City. They were always a highly talented very tough team to play. They were all hearing impaired and played a rough and tumble style of ball. They had players from most of the major cities in Illinois. Some of the boys on their current team were from Chicago, Rockford, Champaign, Quincy and Springfield. They definitely had a wider area of the state to draw students from and the fact they were hearing impaired really had no affect at all on their basketball game because they would never say die, never give up. I.S.D. had a star player named Mehring. How good was Mehring? He was voted the MVP of the entire tournament.

Fortunately the Panthers' defense thwarted their star and held him to only 19 points. Jack Lynn had a great game and scored 32 points. Ashland was victorious and their final score was 67 to 52. Ashland was going to play for the first place trophy.

After Ashland defeated I.S.D., Bowen defeated Astoria. Ashland would face Bowen. Bowen had made it all the way to the Sweet Sixteen where they lost their first game in the State Finals last year. The Panthers would face a big test in Bowen.

Ashland came out strong and took an early lead, but by the end of the first period Bowen had fought back and taken the lead. It was a low scoring defensive struggle for both teams who were in a dead tie at the half 28 to 28. In the beginning of the second half Coach Hoff substituted Glenn Savage for Donny telling him, "Glenn go in there and score some points. Try and give us a lift."

The forward from Bowen fouled Glenn three times in a row while trying to block his shot to keep him from scoring. After Glenn made three free throws in back-to-back fouls the Bowen forward backed away just enough for Glenn to get his jump shot off, and swoosh, it was all net. In less than two minutes at the start of the second half Glenn had accomplished just what Coach Hoff had hoped for; he had scored points and given Ashland the edge. Glenn brought a spark of life from the bench to the team. Coach Hoff put Donny back into the game and the Panthers built their lead to ten points and maintained the lead until the final minute. In the final minute of play, with the game well in hand, the Panthers stood back at the perimeter of the Bowen 2-3 zone defense passing the ball around until time ran out. The score was 60 to 51.

Ashland took home the First Place Trophy in the Astoria Tournament. Donny and Jack were nominated for MVP of the tournament. This game gave the Panthers a boost of confidence. The Panthers were undefeated after winning ten games. They knew they could play with any team and hold their own. Bowen had played in the State Finals and Ashland had defeated them. Jerry Conner said it best in the wrap up of his next sports column, "We went up to Astoria and Zip, Zip, Zip, won all three of our games and brought home the trophy."

Ashland returned to their home court Tuesday night for their eleventh and final game before the Christmas and New Year Holiday's. They were playing the New Berlin Pretzels. The Panthers' spirits were soaring after their first Astoria Championship. Ashland scored on the tip-off and never relinquished the lead. The Panthers held their arms spread eagle in a half court 2-3 zone defense that the New Berlin Pretzels couldn't quite solve.

The strong Ashland defense prevented the New Berlin team from scoring on several occasions. Four Panthers scored in double figures: Donny was the high scorer of the game with 19 points; Denny scored 18; Jack scored 14; and Gary contributed 10 points. They had downed the Pretzels 70 to 50.

The Ashland Panthers had eleven wins and went undefeated into the winter break. They had not gone quietly though because in Illinois at the time there were over 800 high school basketball teams; of those, only 12 schools had teams that remained unbeaten and Ashland was on that short list. Most of those other schools on the list had never heard of Ashland and didn't know where it was.

They had all met at the swimming pool in Elm City last summer and they had been planning this big dance for months. Ronny Jay showed up a little late at Gloria's house. Ronny was in his white dinner jacket and had her corsage, but he and Eddy, Sharon's date, had been drinking beer. That hadn't happened before. Sharon told Eddy off saying, "I won't go to the Snowflake Ball, or dance with you like that."

But Gloria talked her into going anyway if Eddy agreed to stop at the Knotty Pine Café and drink at least two cups of coffee. So they all piled into Ronny's Ford and headed down to the Knotty Pine.

Jack owned a 1949 convertible that was orange and looked like it had been painted by hand with a broom. It had streaks everywhere in the paint. Jerry, Gary, and Jack were cruising around town in Jack's old orange convertible with the top down when Gary had spotted Ronny's car. They pulled into the parking lot at the Knotty Pine and parked right next to Ronny Jay's turquoise and white 1956 Ford Fairlane.

They had followed Ronny from Gloria's house. On the way Gary had shared the whole story about how Ronny Jay was the biggest bully in Elm City. He told them about the first time he ran into him coming home from the pool; he told them about the time Gary busted Ronny's nose; and he told them about the beating they gave him right before he had moved back to Ashland. He told them that Coach Quinn had made Ronny the starting point guard on the Elm City Varsity team when he was a freshman, and Gary always felt he should have had that position. He also told them that Ronny's dad was one of the wealthiest men in Elm City and that as a result Ronny Jay got away with everything he did.

Gary's story about Ronny Jay made Jerry and Jack hot and fighting mad. They were ready to go after Ronny and tear him limb from limb, but Gary who was basically a good kid and never held a grudge calmed them down.

"You know, the guys on my team when we played in your tourney last year are all on the Elm City Varsity with Ronny as their point guard. We may get to play them in the State Finals." Gary said.

"Let's trounce them good." Jerry said.

"We'll score over 100 points and totally embarrass them." Jack said.

"Let's go in and see what my old pal Ronny is up to. Stay cool, calm, and collected. I want to get even with him by beating him on the court." Gary said.

So they went inside for a glass of milk and a piece of homemade apple pie. But Jerry malingered at Ronny's car. He popped the hood admiring Ronny's big V8 engine. Jerry pulled off all eight spark plug wires crossed them in pairs and put them on the sparkplugs. Then Jerry went inside and told Gary and Jack what he'd done. They sat together laughing and laughing and enjoying their milk and pie.

Later that night at the Snowflake Ball Donny Field stood at the entrance of the gym with his date Janet. Donny was handsome in his pink sport coat, black bow tie, gray slacks and white buck suede shoes. He also wore a white carnation on his lapel. Janet had on a fabulous floor length pink pastel gown.

Beautiful snowflakes hung from the ceiling, sparkled everywhere in the gym. The Yachtsmen's Orchestra from Beardstown provided ballroom dance music. Purple and white streamers were attached to a light at the center of the room and mistletoe was hung from the streamers. Christmas trees with lights provided the background for the stage area where the band played.

Everybody in the whole school had helped Pete Gutmann put up the snowflake ornaments and other decorations in the gym. The annual Snowflake Ball was a community project sponsored by all the Ashland High School clubs. Everybody in the sleepy little farm community was invited to the dance. Pete and Marguerite dressed up every year and enjoyed the dance. Mrs. Buker and Mrs. Plattner were Chapter Mothers for the Future Homemakers of America (FHA) and they always served the cookies and punch. But everybody helped all year long with plans, preparations, ornaments and decorations.

This was a formal dance and escorts were expected to wear a coat and a black bow tie. The queen and her court were voted on by an assembly of the student body in early December and they were announced each year by the Master of Ceremonies.

Donny and Janet walked in and said hello to a few people while walking towards Jack and his date Lynell Field, Donny's little sister. Jack who was from a poor family was wearing the same old purple jacket that his dad had worn to the dance so many years before him; Lynell was wearing a gorgeous white strapless gown with lavender trim. Donny said, "Please excuse me. I have to go to the bathroom." And he left unnoticed.

Donny went outside and got into his brand new Nash. Donny lived on a farm and his parents had money. Life always came easy for Donny. He was smart and made good grades without much effort. He always had the newest and best clothes. The State of Illinois gave him a farmer's license when he was 15, and then his parents bought him a new car, a Nash. It had been the demonstrator model and they bought it at a discount. In January of 1956, while Donny was a sophomore, he traded his little brown bomber in for the newest factory model Nash Rambler.

Donny's new Nash had front seats that would go down into a bed. In July when he had taken Janet on a date to the Drive-in Movie Theater over at Elm City, they couldn't get in to see the movie because the Drive-in had a policy against cars that had seats that went down into beds.

Donny drove his new Nash over to pick up Darlene and bring her to the dance. Donny was handsome, easy going and a great basketball player, but sometimes his good nature got him into big trouble. Tonight he had two dates for the Snowflake Ball, and neither girl was aware he had two dates. Janet was his new girlfriend this year and he had asked her to go to the dance. Then Darlene, Donny's girlfriend from last year, came home from Illinois State University and asked him to take her to the dance. They were informally engaged to be married; they had said yes, but weren't telling anybody until Donny graduated in 1958.

Donny didn't have the heart to say no to Darlene, or to tell Janet he couldn't escort her to the dance, so he decided to take them both. He thought he could get away with it without either of his dates ever finding out, and he almost did.

Back at the Snowflake Ball Gary and Jerry arrived. They both had on vanilla colored jackets with colorful little threads of red, purple, and blue splashed around on them. Gloria and Sharon came to the dance a little later, wearing formals, but without their escorts. Sharon had asked Gary, and they were dancing. Gloria asked Jerry, and they were dancing. After their first dance ended. Gary and Sharon, and, Jerry and Gloria stood around and ate punch and cookies.

"What happened to your earlier escorts?" Gary asked.

"They had car trouble. Their car started to cough, sputter and backfire." Gloria said.

"Yeah it sounded like firecrackers going off." Sharon said.

"So what did they do?" Jerry asked.

"Ronny called his dad, and he was sending a tow truck for them." Gloria said.

"What a shame!" Gary and Jerry said simultaneously.

"I didn't want to go with them anyway, they both had been drinking." Sharon said.

"I know those guys from Elm City." Gary said.

"I hope we get a chance to play against them in the finals." Jerry said.

"If we make it to the sectionals we could play them." Gary said.

"They seemed all right when we met them at the swimming pool last summer." Gloria said.

"I'll never go out with them again." Sharon said.

"That's funny! I met them coming home from the swimming pool when I was eleven. I'd like to have heard their car misfiring." Gary said.

"Oh, me too!" Jerry said.

Then they both started laughing ridiculously.

"You guys....did you have something to do with it?" Gloria said, and they all began laughing.

Wallace Wheeler was the Master of Ceremonies. Everybody at school called him Wally. He was an excellent guard and forward on the Varsity basketball team. Wally was the President of the Student Council, and he also was the FHA Chapter Boyfriend. All the Girls loved him. He was the person they chose to stand up at the microphone to announce who had been elected for queen and her court.

"Our new queen for the 'Class of 1957' is Gloria Gerdes." Wally said into the microphone. Everybody in the gym was applauding the announcement.

The other candidates standing there were: Barbara Buker, Marjorie Duncan, Donna Strubbe, and Sharon Forman. When Gloria heard her name she tearfully went forward to receive her crown.

Gloria knew how to have fun. She was a riot to be with. Everybody loved her and thought of her as their friend. Earlier in the week Gloria had been written about in the newspaper because she had been selected as the Betty Crocker Homemaker of Tomorrow. Her essay on homemaking knowledge and attitudes was entered in the All-American Homemaker of Tomorrow, a nation wide competition, and it had been selected as the number one entry in Illinois. For her achievement she received an award pin designed by Trifari of New York. Gloria was the head Cheerleader, Betty Crocker Homemaker of Tomorrow, and she was elected queen of the Snowflake Ball.

Little Becky Quinley, the Chapter Sister, dressed in a pink formal, carried a bouquet of red roses to Gloria. Her escort was Ronny Hoagland, and he carried other small gifts for the queen and her court.

Dennis Bast was the queen's escort, and he was the President of the "Class of 1957." As much as one and all loved Wally, Denny was the star of the basketball team that shined with the most brilliance. Not only did he have the coolest old jalopy in Ashland, with a neat trunk that opened into a rumble seat, but he was also as handsome as any movie star. He was a good kid from a good family. His dad owned and edited the "Ashland Sentinel." Denny was built solidly. He was 6'1" with a muscular physique and weighed 180 pounds soaking wet.

Currently Denny held the school record for the most points scored in a game at 38. Denny was the President of the Lettermen's Club. And to top it all off, every girl in town was in love with him. Denny was a hunk. He was the reason all the girls in town went to the basketball games. Denny was the only player on the team with long wavy dark brown hair. Dennis Bast was a dreamboat.

Right after Gloria was announced the new queen by Wally, Gloria and Denny walked down out to the middle of the gym floor and danced there alone under the light and the mistletoe. Everybody in the whole town stood there watching them dance. At the end of the dance they kissed. Everybody waited for the queen and all of her court to dance as part of their traditional ceremony. There was always a large crowd at the Ball because it was Ashland High School's way of expressing Christmas greetings to the community.

Jack and Lynell were high school sweethearts. They had been going steady since Lynell's first week of classes her freshmen year. When she and Janet went into the bathroom together Darlene was standing in front of the mirror putting on lipstick.

"You both have identical corsages." Lynell said.

Although, it was an innocent enough statement and Lynell had no thought of malice, she had blurted out what she said without thinking. There were dire consequences.

"They are lovely flowers aren't they?" Janet said.

"Donny gave them to me..." Darlene said.

"Donny gave mine to me too..."Janet said.

They looked at the corsages, and looked at each other, and then they both burst out crying at the same time. Janet went out and made Donny take her home. Donny apologized on his way home and talked Janet into forgiving him and they were sweethearts for the rest of 1957. He later went back and took Darlene home. He broke off their secret engagement. Darlene would soon be going back to school at Illinois State University in Normal, Illinois.

After the dance Jerry and Gary were in the back seat of Jack's old orange convertible. Jack was going over to Lynell's house. Lynell told them what had happened in the bathroom.

"Can you believe that guy?" Jack said.

They all laughed.

"What a suave ladies man?" Jerry said.

"And he thought he could get away with it." Gary said.

Pulling up in front of Donny and Lynell's farm Jack said, "Gary you can drive my car around town for a while. Lynell will drive me home later. Just make sure you have the car home by midnight. That's my dad's curfew. Don't keep it out all night like you did the last time I let you use it."

Gary drove away with Jerry and they both went home to change. They were going to drive around to all of the places they new in town to see if they could catch any of the other guys on their ball team out parking. Victory Drive was a favorite place, but tonight it was empty.

They caught Barb Buker and L.E. Stribling parked underneath the old maple at the edge of the baseball field north of the school. They pulled up quietly in front them with their lights off. Gary started flashing the headlights as fast as he could, and both he and Jerry were yelling at them. They caught Marjorie Duncan and David Winklemann next, but none of them were ball players.

Finally they caught Graham Rieken a second team guard on their Varsity team. They were in the parking lot of the "Softie" ice-cream drive-in that was closed for the winter. Graham was in the backseat with Donna Stubbe and when they both sat up she was wearing her bra.

"Hey Graham, you know the coach doesn't allow us to have ice-cream." Jerry said.

"Drop dead." Donna said, pulling her sweater back on.

Gary and Jerry were cruising around when they saw a car they hadn't seen in town before. Ronny Jay and Eddy pulled up beside them.

"We came back to even up the score for what you did tonight. You guys shouldn't have messed with Ronny's new car." Eddy said.

"If you're not too chicken Pearneo, follow us." Ronny said.

They were in Eddy's souped up hot rod. It was a two tone blue 1952 Chevy with 327 V8; it had red flames painted on the fenders coming out from behind the front wheels. They roared out of town for a couple of miles, and then turned down a lonesome dirt road out in the middle of barren farm land. Gary and Jerry followed and pulled in right behind them.

"We'll go up a half mile and turn around. When we flash our lights then you start coming up the middle of the road. We'll be coming at you as fast as we can." Ronny Said.

"The first one to pull off the road is chicken." Eddy said.

He revved up his engine and roared away up the road. Gary gunned the engine. They watched as the 1952 Chevy turned and flashed their lights. Both cars started racing in the middle of the road toward each other. They got closer and closer until they were only about ten feet apart and Gary swerved off the road to his left. The car shot across a three foot ditch and roared up into the air and landed on all four wheels in a plowed field that was ankle deep in soft mud. When the car landed it crashed down so hard Gary's door flew open and he was thrown part of the way out of the car, but his foot got caught and his ankle was badly sprained. At the same time Jerry's head hit the metal dashboard so hard the blow knocked Jerry unconscious.

Ronny and Eddy had swerved and spun around on the road but had not suffered any injuries. They drove by Gary slowly and laughed at him as they pulled away heading back to Elm City. After a few seconds Jerry regained consciousness. Other than Gary's sprained right ankle, and Jerry's lump on his forehead there were no serious injuries or damages.

"Are you okay?" Gary asked.

"Yeah I'm fine. I've got a lump on my head, but I'll put some ice on it when I get home. I'll be fine. How about you?" Jerry asked.

"Oh, not so lucky I guess. I've sprained my right ankle. You'll have to drive." Gary said.

Jerry looked at the mud around the tires and walked to the nearest farm house, roused the farmer out of bed and got him to pull the car out of the field with his tractor.

The farmer laughed and said, "I sure do enjoy watching you boys play basketball. I hope you keep playing as good as you have been."

"We're going all the way this year. We may meet up with the boys that ran us off the road in a ball game and if we do look out." Gary said.

"Those guys are from Elm City." Jerry said.

"Win one for me will you boys?" The farmer said, driving away on his tractor. The farmer had played basketball for the Panthers back in 1920 when he had gone to school with their parents.

"I can't wait to get those guys on the basketball court." Gary said.

"I know we can handle them. Look at how easily we beat them last year when you were on their team." Jerry said.

Jerry drove back into Ashland and dropped Gary off at his house.

"Put some ice on that ankle Gary." Jerry said.

"I will. You know what....? I want to beat Elm City so bad I can taste it. I hope we do eventually get to play them; it would be like killing two bad birds with one stone. I'd love to knock Ronny Jay and Coach Quinn out of the State Tournament, and be the guy who gives them their comeuppance."

The first game of the New Year was Friday, January 4th. The Panthers were playing Chapin. This is what Jerry wrote in his column about the game, "Gary Pearn was unable to suit up due to a badly sprained right ankle, and Wally Wheeler played guard the entire game. Ashland's showing was poor in the first half. The Panthers appeared to be a bit rusty after a long vacation, but they came back in the third period and got their run-and-gun style of play really going strong. Denny, Jack and Donny all shot in double figures; Jerry and Wally both made 8 points. Denny was the high scorer for the night with 27 points. The final score was Ashland 82 Chapin 62. With that victory Ashland has won their 12th straight game of the 1957 season. Out of more than 800 high school basketball teams in Illinois only five teams remain undefeated: Collinsville, Herrin, La Grange, Easton and Ashland."

Chapter 8

It happened this fall after their third game of the season. Coach Hoff was in a rush to get home and left school early and he caught Jim Ratliff with a lit cigarette in his hand and saw him blowing smoke out of his mouth. Jim was leaning against a tree. Coach Hoff got into his car and drove by Jim; he rolled his window down and told him to see him in his office first thing the next morning. In the morning Coach Hoff told him he wouldn't allow anybody on the Varsity team to smoke, and that he was kicked off the basketball team.

Jim Ratliff never did tell anybody at school what happened. When anybody on the team asked about his absences he just told them he didn't like basketball very much and that he really didn't miss those tough workouts Coach Hoff put them through. The team was having such a great season that after a couple of weeks nobody noticed he was gone.

One week following the Panthers game with Chapin Coach Hoff was riding rough shod over the team in practices because he didn't want them to have a mid-season let down. Gary's ankle was sore, but it was beginning to heal up enough that he could practice. Bob Savage, a forward on the team, had let his dad drive his car that day because his dad had some important out of town business. When Bob's dad arrived early to pick him up he parked Bob's car in the lot where Coach Hoff and the team normally parked their cars.

Bob drove a beautiful bronze 1957 Chevy Bel-Air. Mr. Savage was sitting on the driver's side, and he was listening to music on the radio while he waited for his son Bob to finish basketball practice. Coach Hoff, who was very tired from a hard day of working out with the basketball team, went home early again right after sending the team into the locker room for their showers.

Coach Hoff got into his red and white 1954 Chevy started the motor and as he began driving out of the parking lot he glanced into his rearview mirror as he slowly pulled away. He saw the reddish glow of a cigarette burning in the hand of a dark shadowy person in Bob Savage's car. It was dark and Coach Hoff couldn't quite make out who he saw in his mirror that night. But one thing was certain, he saw the reddish glow of a cigarette burning in the hand of the person in that car. Since it was Bob's car, Coach Hoff assumed it was Bob Savage he saw there in the dark smoking.

Appropriately, the next morning Coach Hoff called Bob down to his office, "You don't need to come to practice anymore." Coach Hoff said bluntly and with no explanation. Bob walked out of his office in shock. At the next basketball practice Coach Hoff told the team, "I had to kick Bob off the team." That news dampened their team spirit considerably. The prominence of his absence was immediately conspicuous; of course, all of Bob's teammates knew Bob never smoked, but they didn't understand that Bob was kicked off the team for smoking. It made practice difficult because when Bob was there they had a pretty solid second team. Bob and his cousin Glenn Savage, Ed Birch, Graham Rieken and Wally Wheeler, made a fine second team for the Ashland Varsity. Bob made the team have an even number—ten players on the Varsity team.

If Bob, Glenn, or Wally had played for any other high school team in the state they probably would have been on the starting team. As it was they sat on the bench a lot waiting for their numbers to be called. With Bob off the team it not only weakened their team depth to nine men, but Coach Hoff had to try and play in his place during scrimmages when the first team played the second team in practice. Ernie Hoff was a pretty outstanding basketball player, but he was no Bob Savage. In every aspect of the game of basketball Bob Savage was a better player than Hoff.

After three days of confusion and wondering what possible reason Coach Hoff had for kicking him off the team, Bob went to see Superintendent Bierman in his office.

"Come in Bob and sit down. I understand you want to talk to me about Coach Hoff?" Mr. Bierman said.

"Yes Sir, Coach Hoff called me down to his office and kicked me off the basketball team without explaining why; and for the past three days I've been wondering what his reason was." Bob said.

"You say Coach Hoff kicked you off the team without any explanation?" Mr. Bierman asked.

"That's right Sir—I don't care whether I'm done playing on the team or not, but I at least want to know the reason why." Bob said.

"Wait here one minute. I'll be right back Bob." Mr. Bierman said.

Mr. Bierman walked out of his office and down the hall into Coach Hoff's office.

"Good morning Ernie." Mr. Bierman said.

"Good morning Bruno. What brings you down here to my office on such a fine day?" Coach Hoff said.

"I'd like to have a minute of your time if I could. Can you walk with me to my office? Mr. Bierman asked.

"Sure, I'd be glad to." Coach Hoff said.

They began walking back to Superintendent Bierman's office. Mr. Bierman was a pretty big sized guy. He had a gentle face with a dimpled chin. His hair and eyebrows were white. The top of his head was totally bald and very shiny. He always wore new suits with the latest style of colorful tie. He was an extremely fair man who believed in talking with people, getting to the bottom of things and working out problems reasonably and rationally. When they arrived at Mr. Bierman's office he asked Coach Hoff to listen to what Bob had to say.

"I'd like to know the reason you kicked me off the team." Bob said.

"You know my rules. Anybody caught smoking is off the team. I saw you three nights ago, in your bronze car after practice." Coach Hoff said.

"Coach I let my dad use the car for some out of town business and he came to practice to pick me up. It was my dad you saw smoking, not me. I don't smoke." Bob said.

"Is your father home now?" Mr. Bierman asked.

"I think so." Bob said.

"What's your phone number Bob?" Mr. Bierman asked, picking up the black phone on his desk.

"3-3-2-7." Bob said, and Mr. Bierman dialed the number.

"Mr. Savage, I'm sorry to bother you. This is Mr. Bierman calling from Ashland High School. I'd like to ask you a couple of questions....Were you driving Bob's car last Monday night....? Yes, good, now were you sitting in the school parking lot smoking....? You were, oh fine, Mr. Savage. I hope to see you at the basketball games next week. Thank you! Goodbye." Mr. Bierman said on the phone.

"Bob's dad just confirmed everything Bob just said. Is it possible that you saw Bob's dad smoking and thought it was Bob?" Mr. Bierman asked.

"Bob I'm sorry. It was your bronze car and I thought it was you." Coach Hoff said.

Bob laughed and said, "A lot of people tell me that I look like my dad."

"If you'll come back to practice, and I hope you will because the team needs you—and give it 110%, I'll forget this ever happened. Coach Hoff said, holding his hand out and shaking hands with Bob.

"Thanks Coach, I love playing basketball. Thanks Mr. Bierman." Bob said and he walked out of the office, went down the hall and back into his classroom.

"Thanks for clearing this matter up for us Bruno." Coach Hoff said.

"I'm glad I could help. Bob is a great kid and you've got a wonderful team....Are you hungry? I'm hungry, why don't we walk down to the cafeteria and I'll ask Mrs. Buker to make us a sandwich and we can have a cup of coffee."

Ernie and Bruno were seen often walking to the cafeteria together for coffee and a mid-morning or mid-afternoon snack. They were good friends.

That evening Bob Savage suited up for practice. Gary's sore foot was almost completely healed and he also suited up for practice. For the rest of the 1957 season none of the ten boys that made up the Varsity team missed a practice, or a game. They all were trying their best to help the team go as far as they could. Momentum and excitement was building and they all worked very hard in their practices. From that time forward the whole team began to flourish and show signs of greatness.

Basketball was becoming the main social event in the sleepy little farm community of Ashland.

One man sharpens another like iron. The level of play the team brought to practice the next few days was exceptional. The whole team was on fire. They were explosive and dynamic. Jack Lynn played the true center position as well as anybody in the state. On the rare, unlikely occasion when he would foul out then Donny would shift up and Wally would come into the game and the team would pick up the pace with three guards, Denny at forward, as always, and Donny playing center. How it came to be that all these great players came from one of the tiniest farm communities in Illinois nobody ever really knew. There wasn't a team in the whole state that could match up with them man-for-man.

That week in practice the team was preparing for the coming 29th Ashland Tournament. Coach Hoff had the team spread out on the floor with hands above elbows and elbows above waists. Then at Coach Hoff's command they would slide left, right, forward, back and diagonal. They practiced those in every practice. They had two defenses, man-to-man, and zone. They played zone in their games almost all the time. The two half court zone defenses they utilized the most were 2-3 and the 2-1-2. In the 2-1-2 Gary and Jerry their great guards, would be up front; then in the middle was their intimidating center Jack; behind him came the two outstanding forwards, Donny and Denny. In the 2-3 it was usually Gary and Jerry out front and Denny, Jack and Donny in back.

Rarely, they used two other half court zone defenses 3-2 and the 4-1. The 3-2 was exceptionally intimidating against small teams because Jack would come out front and stand between Gary and Jerry. Jack weighed 180 pounds and was 6'4" with very long arms. He was also the best jumper on the team with a 40 inch vertical leap. He almost always won the tip-off at the beginning of the game. Gary was 5'9" and the lightest and quickest player on the team. He weighed 142. Jerry was 5'10" and weighed 165. Behind them in the 3-2 were Denny who was 6'1" and weighed 180, and Donny who was 6'3" and weighed 175. The two forwards would be in back with their long arms extended. Denny Bast, their forward was far and away the best all around shooter and athlete on their team. He played the game with such ease, but when they all took the floor together their game was magical.

The 4-1, or the box-and-one defense was used only twice all year, and then only for two or three minutes as a change of pace. In the box- and-one, Gary played the ball; he went where-ever the ball was. The other four men Jerry and Denny, Jack and Donny played in a square, stationary zone with their arms extended. While they collapsed into their packed in zone defense the offense couldn't get a shot off because Gary was always there smothering the ball handler. Gary was so quick and had so much speed that he would scoop the ball away with his left hand. When he would steal the ball, then Jerry or Denny would fast-break toward the other end of the court. Jerry knew exactly when Gary was going to make his move to steal a ball. Ball players that Gary guarded didn't know he was left handed and ambidextrous. Gary sometimes could steal as many as 12 balls a game.

Gary would steal the ball and make a baseball pass to Jerry or Denny and they would go in for an easy lay-up. It would happen so fast two or three times in a row that it would unnerve any rival. The major flaw with that defense was that when Gary ran full tilt sprinting after the ball for an extended period of time it would severely wear him down and that would diminish his overall game. After playing the box-and-one defense Coach Hoff always had to take Gary out of the Game for a minute to rest, catch his breath and get his heart-rate back to normal. It was the most difficult defense because it would simply overwork any ballplayer. The team didn't use it very often.

"The Prohibitive Favorites" was what Jerry wrote in his sports article about Ashland and their 29th Tournament. The Ashland team was so good that a year earlier when Coach Hoff had invited 12 schools only three accepted. So just like last year when Gary played for Elm City there would be four teams in the Ashland Tournament: St. Mary's from Mount Sterling, Routt a team from Elm City, and Tallula. The tournament was better this year because they were all good Varsity teams.

In 1957 the Ashland Invitational was the second oldest tournament in the state. The Winchester tournament was the other one. They both started in 1922. Winchester had their tournament every year, but from 1950-1955 Ashland had a hiatus. After Ernie Hoff resumed the tournament his first year as coach, then excitement for basketball was growing in the community so much that on game night everybody in town went to see the Panthers play basketball. The crowds began to show up an hour before game time and they were bringing picnic baskets.

When the Ashland Invitational began in 1922 it was five years before the Panthers had a team good enough to win their own tournament. Ashland had won their own tournament eleven times, starting from 1928, then they didn't win again until five more years had passed, and then they won it for seven consecutive years from 1933-1939. Four years later they won again in 1944 and 1945. Most of the players on the current team went to see the 1944-1945 Ashland Panthers play, although they would have been five or six years old. Ashland didn't win again for 11 years until they brought the trophy home again in 1956.

In the first game of the 29th Invitational Ashland easily put the game away against St. Mary's. Feeling his ankle was 100% Gary played exceptionally well handling the ball with ease. The entire team was hot and all five starting players scored in double figures. Half way through the third period the first team sat on the bench and watched as the second team finished the game. Ashland won 87 to 46. Jerry was the high scorer with 23 points. That night everybody on the team scored. The second team players scores were: Wally 12, Bob 9, Glenn 8, Edgar 6, and Graham came off the bench to contribute 3 points. After that Routt downed Tallula.

Two days later the Ashland Panthers played the Routt Rockets a Catholic High School from Elm City for the championship game. The Panthers took an early lead and easily controlled the Rockets. Ashland played steady and maintained their lead the whole game. The final score was 63 to 45. Denny led the attack with 17 points, Jack 13, Gary 12, Donny 11, Jerry 8, Wally 2. In both these games the starters had begun to balance their scoring attack. In their future games, a well balanced offensive attack mixed with a tough defensive full court press zone would give their opponent's coaches headaches. That was the second year in a row that Ashland brought home the trophy 1956 and 1957; and that was the 12th time Ashland won first place.

Increasingly, Gary's confidence was growing with each game he played. He was always coming up with a new and different move. The fans, the coach, and the entire team enjoyed watching him play basketball. With the passage of time Gary steadily performed at higher levels. Gary's athleticism had helped contribute to the Panthers winning streak; the Panthers had won 14 consecutive games.

In their next game, Ashland opened up with their full court zone press and crushed Pleasant Plains. The score at the end of the first half was 61 to 24. The game ended with the score 91 to 61. Again all the starters scored in double figures led by Jack with 28 points. The victory elevated the Panthers to their 15th win.

At that point Denny and Jack were unquestionably the dominant shooters on the floor, but all five of the starters were definite scoring threats to their opponents. Coaches and teams began to try to figure out new and creative ways to try and stop Denny and Jack from scoring. They also had one of the toughest 2-3 half court zone defenses in the state. When they unleashed that terrible full court zone press defense then no team in the state could get half way down court with the basketball. They usually turned the ball over and the Panthers would score again before they got to the center of the court. When the Panthers were hot at shooting, they could shoot from anywhere on the court. Gary could jump up over any defender and release a shot a couple of steps from the center court that went in without touching the rim. On the other hand Donny could deliver a mean and ugly looking hook shot from anywhere on the floor that would bang on the rim, hit up against the backboard, then roll three times around the rim, but somehow it would find its way into the hoop. Waxing poetic one day Coach Hoff told Donny, "Your shots were crazy, but they helped us win, no matter how you got it away, it would finally roll in."

Then there was Jerry Conner who was tough and scrappy and always found a way to contribute excellent shots. Jerry was a small guy from a very small school. From an early age Jerry had a bit of an inferiority complex. He was poor, he was small, and to make things worse he had worn thick lenses in his glasses since he was nine years old. He never had a problem with a big head because he always tended to think the worst of himself. Jerry was a tough and scrappy guy who had more fight and desire in him than actual talent.

Desire was a main ingredient for success in any sport. Jerry worked very hard to get to the level of play he was at as a guard for the Panthers. He always thought his greatest achievement in life was how he succeeded in becoming the starting guard on the Varsity when he was a sophomore in high school. He was the type of guy that if he got knocked down, he got up and was more aggressive than ever. When he made the starting team his sophomore year, he left a lot of the bigger kids sitting on the bench.

Jerry's next sports report said, "In last night's game Ashland used a zone defense to baffle the I.S.D. Tigers from Elm City. The Panthers again were in the lead from start to finish. The scores were: 26-12 the first period, and 45-21 by half time. In the third period the Panthers zone held I.S.D. to 4 points. A good floor showing helped Ashland swamp I.S.D. The final score was 80 to 42. Donny led the scoring with 27 points. The Ashland Panthers were beginning to look invincible." The victory gave Ashland their 16th win and a lot of confidence going into their next important home game with Easton.

Chapter 9

Elm City was a short sixteen miles from Ashland. Tonight Easton was going to play Ashland on Ashland's home floor. Gary's mom and little brother rode the train from Elm City to Ashland to watch Gary play point guard in the game. Gary's brother who was almost six years old was very excited about getting to see his brother again. It was his first train ride and it was the first time he would watch his big brother play basketball with the Panthers.

Gary's little brother would always remember the sounds and the steady rhythm of the train's wheels on the steel tracks. He felt safe sitting next to his mother. The countryside was magnificently covered with a foot of snow and around the edges the train's windows were coated with frost. He listened to his mom's wonderful voice; he loved her Texas accent. She told him the story about her very first train ride with her mom and dad when she was seven years old.

"I was almost your age when I went on my first train ride with your Grandma and Grandpa Weaver. I sat beside my sisters Eda Mae and Marguerite. We came from the Texas Panhandle in 1920 when all the dust was really bad, and we rode all the way to Ashland. I'll always remember the first time I saw the Mississippi River when the train crossed over the bridge. Sunlight sparkled and danced on the water. It was so beautiful."

Gary's little brother had inherited his mom's big curls, strawberry blond hair and blue eyes. Gary and his sisters, Donna, Phyllis and Sara Jane, whom Gary always affectionately called "Janie," had all inherited their dad's dark brown hair color.

Gary sure was glad to see his mom and brother again at the big game. And it was a big game for Ashland because last year the Easton team had beaten Ashland in two of their four losses. Easton had knocked them out of the state tournament, so the Panthers were laying low for the Easton game. Also, last year and up until now the Panthers were undefeated on their home floor and they wanted to keep that streak going tonight.

Easton entered the game undefeated with 14 victories; Ashland entered the game also undefeated with 16 victories. Two other teams were undefeated Herrin and Collinsville. People all across Illinois were interested in this game to find out which team would remain undefeated. With an hour to go before game time there were spectators standing around the bleachers that were packed full to overflowing. The parking lots were overflowing and people were parking on both sides of the streets for a mile up the road both directions. Sports writers from Springfield, Elm City and Peoria had descended on Ashland were in the stands to cover the big game that was also being broadcast on Radio by WLDS-FM.

Gary was in the locker room putting on his white uniform with purple trim. In the locker room next door the Easton Hawks were putting on their dark blue uniforms with yellow trim. Gary hadn't realized it yet, but he had a tenacious facet in his character. The tougher things got the harder he tried. The more tired he felt the faster he would run. When the competition was the stiffest, most gut wrenching and nerve wracking, it was then that Gary would get into a zone and find that sweet spot where everything seemed to go in slow motion around him. Tonight he would find that sweet spot from the first tip-off until the final seconds of the game.

The crowd roared as the Panthers took the floor. Jack led the team sprinting as fast as they could out the tunnel around the floor dribbling basketballs. They circled back to their basket and each player made a lay-up except Donny and Jack who both dunked the ball rattling the rim, shaking the backboard and intimidating the Hawks. At the beginning of the game Jack tipped the ball to Donny who tossed it quickly back to Jack and he scored the first two points of the game on an easy lay-up.

The game was close all the way. With two minutes before the first half ended the Hawks had taken the lead and were building it. The score was Hawks 47 Panthers 43. The Hawks had the ball bringing it up court and were threatening to build a six point lead when Gary cut in front of a pass from Hoffman intended for Knight. At the same moment that Gary intercepted the ball Denny began to sprint leading the fast-break down floor where he was all alone. Gary passed the ball to Denny who made an easy five foot jumper.

This time when the Hawks brought the ball up the floor Gary went out to meet the guy dribbling the basketball, Gary scooped the ball away with his left hand and tossed it to Jerry. Jerry held the ball up letting the Hawks get set in their 2-3 zone and then threw the ball to Donny. In the last seconds of the half Donny threw up a crazy hook shot that went in and at the half the score was tied up 47 to 47.

In the third period the tough hard fought battle resumed. The Hawks regained the lead and never looked back building it to eight points. In the fourth period Gary and the Panthers slowly scratched and clawed their way back into the game; and then, Easton came back and tied the score at 86 to 86. Gary had the ball; Coach Hoff called a timeout and put Bob Savage into the game in place of Jerry. Gary told Bob, "Watch for the ball, when I pass it to you shoot it."

Bob made the jump shot and they regained the lead 88 to 86. Then the Hawks scored on a shot by Jackson and tied it 88 to 88. Gary dribbled down across the center line. Normally at this point he would pass the ball away, but instead he did a little head bobble-d-boop and went around the man guarding him like he was standing still, and Gary fired a jump shot that went in. The score was 90 to 88. The crowd went wild. But as time was running out the Hawks threw the ball up court without dribbling and Jackson scored quicker than you could blink an eye. The game ended 90 to 90 and went into a five minute overtime period. Coach Hoff's conditioning really paid off in the game because the Hawks looked worn and haggardly in the beginning of overtime, but the Panthers were ready to turn it up a notch, and they really turned on the steam in the final minutes.

Jack tipped the ball to Jerry in the overtime. Jerry passed it to Donny and Donny passed it to Denny and Denny gave it back to Jack who scored the first two points in overtime. The crowd went wild again. This time up the floor Jackson missed and Jack got the rebound. He was fouled and made both free throw shots bringing the score to 94 to 90. Then Easton scored two points and it was 94 to 92. Denny made the next basket for Ashland and the score was 96 to 92. With ten seconds left Hoffman scored a basket for the Hawks and they were within two points at 96 to 94. Then Gary threw the ball in to Bob and the Hawks fouled Bob to stop the clock with three seconds. Bob made one basket at the free throw line and the Hawks had the ball in the final few seconds, but the Panthers smothered them defensively and they never got a shot off. Ashland won the game 97 to 94. Denny was the high scorer for the game with 26 points. Ashland was one of three undefeated teams in Illinois and the whole community was celebrating.

"Squawk, two birds with one stone. Two birds with one stone. Kill two birds with one stone." Gary's pet parrot said.

Gary laughed as he got out of bed at 6:00 A.M. At the start of his school year Gloria Gerdes had taken Gary's snapshot for the yearbook, and asked him what clubs he had participated in at Elm City. As a joke Gary threw in "Bird Watching Club." Jerry Conner had been sitting beside him at the time he said it. They were in study hall. Gloria wrote it down without question and put it in the yearbook along with all of his other club activities, but Jerry and Gary nearly died laughing when she left the classroom. They laughed so hard that their teacher, Coach Hoff had to send them down to the gym to shoot free throws because they were disrupting everybody's studying.

On January 10, 1957 Gary turned eighteen, and as a joke, the guys on the basketball team, including Coach Hoff and the manager Bob McCarthy pooled their money and Jerry and Denny went to Springfield and bought Gary a parrot for his birthday present. They gave it to him right after basketball practice on his birthday. Gary, who hadn't owned a pet since he was a small boy on the farm when he and his older sisters had a piglet as pet, was overwhelmed by the gift. Even though it was meant as a joke Gary loved that parrot. He promptly taught the gorgeous multicolored bird how to say, "Two birds with one stone. Two birds with one stone. Kill two birds with one stone." And the parrot said it every morning at 6:00 A.M. when Gary's alarm clock went off.

Gary was really hoping that his team would make it to the Sweet Sixteen and try to win the state championship. But he was also hoping that Elm City with Coach Quinn and Ronny Jay playing point guard would make it as far as the Sectionals, where if everything went the right way they would meet, and the Cougars would have to play against his Panthers. Gary wanted to beat them and give them their comeuppance. That was why he taught his pet parrot that he named Humphrey Bogart to say what he said every morning.

Every morning Humphrey Bogart said, "Squawk—two birds with one stone. Two birds with one stone. Kill two birds with one stone." And every morning Gary got out of bed laughing, thinking about playing against Elm City in the state play offs. Gary walked to school every morning with a big smile on his face because he was so happy about being able to play basketball at Ashland. And he was fiercely proud of how well his team played basketball. Every morning Jerry met Gary at his dad's house and they walked to school together. Sometimes Sharon joined them.

Most of the girls didn't have cars. A few were allowed to drive their parent's cars, but mostly they walked everywhere in town. Jerry, Gary and Wally didn't have cars of their own and did a lot of walking. Everything was close so that made walking easy and commonplace. A few of the kids who lived out on farms rode the school buses. Since everybody knew everybody else and they were all good friends, if somebody had wheels and saw someone walking, then they would offer them a ride. Gary and Jerry rode around town a lot with Denny in the rumble seat of his old brown jalopy.

Ashland traveled to Balyki for their next conference game; Balyki didn't want to play basketball with them. Their strategy was to execute a continuous stall for four periods. It was a slow paced slow moving game. The Panthers jumped to a quick lead. Jack tipped the ball to Gary who passed it to Donny who made the first two points. The Balyki offense was remarkably unhurried, and became deliberately slower as the game progressed. The score at the end of the first period was 8 to 5. When the Panthers went into the locker room for half time the score was 16 to 9.

In the third and fourth periods the Panthers opened the lead and ran when they could. It was without question the dullest game of the season and the final score was 48 to 24. Donny was the leading scorer with 17 points, and 11 of his points were from free throws. It was the Panthers 18th victory.

Then the Panthers traveled to Greenfield to play the Tigers. The Tigers tried their best to play basketball with the Panthers, but Ashland jumped out to an early lead and held it comfortably all the way. Donny played another great game as they had their fast-break really going, but Donny played a little too aggressive and fouled out in the third period. Coach Hoff told him he could go ahead and shower. Donny left the floor, showered and came back with his blue jeans on, and then sat on the bench and enjoyed watching his team cruise to victory. During the final four minutes the Tigers held the ball to prevent Ashland from scoring 100 points on them. Since they had a big lead they chose not to go out after the ball. The final score was 98 to 52. Jack was the high scorer with 31 points, but Donny, Denny, Jerry, Gary and Wally also scored in double figures for their 19th win.

With all cylinders running full tilt, the Panthers tore through the Chandlerville Comets. They went out to a fast lead and kept building momentum. At half time the score was 44 to 18. The Panthers performance level was peaking, they were playing superior basketball and they looked nearly perfect. Their shots were a thing of beauty to watch, almost poetic. Their passes were snapped quickly and looked sharp. They sprinted up and down the floor leaving other teams in their dust. They played a little too aggressive against the comets though, Jack and Denny fouled out in the fourth period. Donny moved up to center when Wally and Bob came into the game. Both Jerry and Gary played the final period with four fouls.

The final score was 95 to 46. Denny was the high scorer with 29 points and the other four starters also scored in double figures. That game gave the Panthers their 20th victory and their final conference win so they were awarded the West Central Conference Trophy. It was their third first place trophy and they now had trophies from the Astoria Tournament, the Ashland Tournament and their own West Central Conference.

The Virginia Redbirds frustrated by their 1956 loss to Ashland in the game where Jerry dribbled the ball for the entire third period dropped the Panthers from their schedule for the 1957 season. Coach Hoff had replaced the Redbirds with a team from Farmersville.

They had never played Farmersville and didn't quite know what to expect. The game was in an old, shabby, small gym and the floors were grimy and badly in need of a dust mop. In their gym at Ashland the hardwood floor was old, but it was kept clean and shiny by Pete Gutmann who dusted the floor before each game, then again at half time, as well as after each game. The gym at Farmersville smelled musky.

If the Panthers were well oiled machinery, then the Farmersville kids were the exact opposite. Ashland was well disciplined and in excellent condition. Farmersville was undisciplined and out of shape. They had uniforms that were old and didn't match and wore long hair. One kid was playing ball in a pair of cutoff jeans and a baseball jersey. Needless to say, they were all good clean farm kids, but their coach had never been in the US Marines. And there wasn't a true athlete in the bunch. But oh, were they scrappy, nonchalant and had an, "I could care less," attitude.

Coach Hoff called a team huddle right before the tip off and said, "Relax, enjoy the game and have fun. I want try something a little different tonight. I'm going to start the entire second team and I want you guys to forget all the plays we practice. Play man-to-man defense. Bob guard their center, Wally and Glenn I want you guarding their forwards and Graham and Edgar stick with their guards. Now relax, don't worry just go in there and play your best."

The Panthers were mildly surprised by the unexpected change, but they all laughed at the thought of it.

"That scruffy team looks like our J.V. could beat them." Coach Hoff said as the team broke the huddle.

Farmersville took the floor and played a scrappy, tough and unpredictable style of ball, but to no avail. The score at the end of the first period was 22 to 11. By the end of the first half of play the score was 42 to 25. A minute after the start of the third period Bob fouled out. The kid from Farmersville, Bob had been guarding, was bumping and grinding against him all night and for some inexplicable reason the fouls had all gone against Bob. It was just one of those things, but it was too bad for Farmersville because Coach Hoff replaced Bob with Jack.

Jack scored at will every time the Panthers passed the ball to him and they turned up the steam and rolled over Farmersville 87 to 50. It was their 21st victory and Jack was the high scorer with 23 points, all scored in the second half. Wally and Bob both had 19 points, Edgar had 16, and Graham scored 10. That was the high point of the season for the second team, and they picked up a little swagger after the Farmersville game. Jerry, Gary, Denny and Donny sat on the bench the entire game resting, and they laughed, had a great time and absolutely enjoyed cheering for the second team.

Coach Hoff was a great guy, but you didn't want to get him mad. The coach had a terrible mouth. He could cuss a blue streak like nobody from around Ashland had heard before. Probably it was a negative result of his being drafted into the Marines during the Korean War. During practice sometimes it seemed like every other word coming out of his mouth was an extremely bad word.

They say that one bad apple spoils the whole barrel. Well it wasn't too long after the beginning of the 1957 season when all the young athletes on the unmitigated basketball team were cursing all the time. It got so bad that the guys were actually cussing at the dinner table in front of their parents. The parents, who were shocked and appalled by their son's carelessly dirty mouths, formed a group who went to talk with Superintendent Bierman. Mr. Bierman, in response to the parents, asked Coach Hoff to do something to try and curb the use of bad language by the ball team.

The next day at practice Coach Hoff announced that anybody heard cussing would be charged 25 cents for every cuss word he said. And that included the coach. He did that to try and stop everybody from cussing. If somebody cussed and he didn't have the money to pay at the time they were caught, then they could owe that amount until it was paid. Earlier in the season Jack Lynn owed the coach 75 cents because he was having trouble controlling his expletives. When the coach asked him to pay up, Jack handed him a one dollar bill.

"I don't have any change on me." Coach Hoff said.

"Well, son-of-a-______! Just keep the whole thing," Jack said.

Chapter 10

One of the Varsity Cheerleaders, Barb Buker used to swipe love letters out of a desk at study hall, read them, and pass the letters around at lunchtime so everybody else could read them too. And then after everybody had read them, Barb would put the letters right back in the desk.

Buell Meyer, a guy who was a junior, and Alice Sanders who was a senior, were the high school sweethearts who wrote those letters. They were a very affectionate couple in school and everyday at lunchtime they would leave school walking together and holding hands. They would walk down the street to get away from the school grounds where they could hug and kiss romantically. Barb and several other classmates followed them everyday to see where they were going and to watch them making out.

Gary's love for the game of basketball was both real and intense. Four regular season games remained and Ashland played them with intensity because they were confident they could end their regular season undefeated. The Panthers had to travel to White Hall, come home and play Routt, then Elkhart, and travel to Divernon for their final game of the season. Two weeks later the District Tournament would begin. Last year, one of the three teams that defeated Ashland was Elkhart. If Ashland could knock them off they would have managed to get their revenge on all the teams that defeated them in 1956. When Elkhart defeated Ashland in the Championship game of the Williamsville Tournament last year, Elkhart had led by

13 points for most of the game. The Panther's four losses in their 1956 season came against Petersburg, Elkhart, and Easton.

Easton had beaten them twice. The first time it was on Easton's home floor, and the second time it was in the District Championship game on a neutral court over at Chandlerville. All of their losses last year came in games they played on the road. In the 1957 season, although Ashland had previously defeated Easton in Ashland, the Easton Hawks had an advantage in the District Tournament because it was scheduled to be played at Easton. All the games Easton played in the tournament would be on their home floor, in front of all their fans.

After the Panthers played at White Hall Jerry Conner wrote about the game in his weekly column for the "Ashland Sentinel" in it Jerry said, "Ashland rolled over White Hall. Their gym was the smallest the Panthers played in all year. It looked like a cracker box. At half time the score was 44 to 30. Everyone played in the game. The Panthers finished with a score of 76 to 59. Jack was the leading scorer with 22 points, followed closely by Denny with 18 and Gary with 17. Donny contributed 9, Jerry and Wally both put in 4, and Bob added two points."

On February 15, 1957 the Routt Rockets came to Ashland from Elm City. Routt was a scrappy little Catholic High School team. Their school colors were the same as the Panther's purple and white. In the game Ashland wore white uniforms with purple trim and Routt wore purple uniforms with white trim. Routt was a very physical and tenacious team that actually tried to run with the Panthers. They were battling and keeping the game close. Although, Ashland had the game well in hand, Routt was not a team to go down without a fight.

Jack went to the free throw line for 20 attempts. Their strategy seemed to be "foul the big man." Jack made 15 free throws that night and he had a 75% average at the free throw line. Jack was the high scorer for the night with 35 points. The Panthers beat the Rockets that night 84 to 78.

The year 1957 was a great year for old cars. Denny had reddish-brown primer paint on his 1938 Ford Roadster that sported a rumble seat in the trunk. But, Jack's wheels were the wildest. He had a 1949 Chevy convertible that looked like it had been painted with orange house paint.

"The paint job had streaks in it that looked so bad. It looks like it had been hand painted with a broom," Jack said.

Both Edgar and Glenn drove green Chevy's; Edgar's was a 1949 model, and Glenn's was a newer 1951 model. The Panther's Manager Bob McCarthy drove the most unique car of them all. A 1951 black Packard that was an old hearse he had purchased at a real bargain from a funeral parlor director. It was beautiful and like new; it was as big as a limousine with three bench seats in the back that had never been sat on. In fact, the seats were in storage when Bob bought the hearse. Bob's car could comfortably seat the entire ball team.

Bob used to take a carload of ballplayers over to Pleasant Plains to go bowling and it would cause quite a stir. The Panthers were famous all around central Illinois in 1957. Whenever the team went to another town in Bob's hearse everybody would recognize them and call them by name. It made the players feel great. They had a lot of confidence in themselves. The whole town of Ashland was very proud of their team. The Panthers were the exciting talk of the town and the neighboring towns were also talking about them. When the players and the cheerleaders went rolling into a nearby town in that black hearse, everybody knew who they were, and everybody that saw them would smile, wave and cheer them on.

The year 1957 was a great year for new cars too. The all time favorite car from that year was the Chevrolet Bel-Air. Two Panther's were fortunate enough to drive that new model 1957 Chevy. Graham Rieken had a brown and white version that had been displayed on the dealer's showroom floor as a demonstrator. Bob Savage had one too, his had a beautiful bronze finish.

Another extremely popular new car that year was the Nash Rambler. In fact, there was a popular song about a race between a Nash and a Cadillac, and the tiny Nash won. If Bob McCarthy owned the biggest car in town, then Donny Field's car was the smallest because he drove a tiny Nash. Donny was given his first new Nash Rambler by his parents when he was 15 years old. In January of 1956 while he was a sophomore, he traded his little brown bomber in for a brand new Nash Rambler that had seats that would fold back into a bed. But what distinguished Donny's car from all the others was his fantastic factory ordered paint job. Donny convinced his parents to let him drive all the way up to the factory to pick up his new car because he would save money picking it up at the factory. While all the other 1957 Nash Ramblers were in two tone colors like light and dark blue, or light and dark green, Donny's Nash was brilliantly painted two colors, purple and white.

It was really something to see when all of the Ashland Panthers drove all their different and unique cars to the school parking lot and parked and went into the gym to play their final home game of the year. Elkhart had come into town, in their big yellow school buses, ready to do what no other team had been able to do to the Ashland Panthers all year long, they were planning to break the Panthers full court zone press defense and beat them.

The Panthers had another idea though, about how their final home game of the year should be played. Denny was ready for Elkhart and he was more fired up than anybody had ever seen him before; in the first period every shot he put up went through the hoop. Denny shot 100% from the field and he had really found his sweet spot. It was perfect. At the end of the first period the score was 28 to 9. They really had the Ashland fans cheering wildly. The Panthers were pounding the boards and continued to build their lead the entire first half. At the half time break the score was Ashland 57, Elkhart 22.

Elkhart was in shock. They didn't know what had hit them. By the end of the third period the Panthers were leading 73 to 32. Coach Hoff loved it and felt so confident about winning that at the beginning of the fourth period he began to bring his first team out of the game.

He did it methodically bringing one player out at a time. The audience gave each one of them a standing ovation. The first player he brought out was Donny because he was the youngest, and he received a standing ovation, and Bob Savage went in to play for him right after the fourth period began. Donny put on his warm up uniform and sat down on the bench to enjoy the game.

Next the coach brought out Jerry who received a standing ovation, and he put on his warm up uniform and sat down beside Donny on the bench. Wally Wheeler went into the game to play when Jerry came out. Then the coach took Jack out, and he received a standing ovation. Jack put on his warm up uniform and sat down beside Jerry. Glenn Savage went into the game for Jack. Then coach brought Gary out of the game and Gary received a standing ovation. Gary's eyes began to tear up with joy over what he had accomplished that year. Gary put on his warm ups and sat down on the bench beside Jack as Edgar Birch went into the game. Finally Coach Hoff brought out their team leader and Captain Denny and everybody stood up and cheered for Denny. He put on his warm ups and sat down on the bench beside Gary. Graham Rieken went onto the floor to play.

Coach Hoff had timed each substitution approximately one minute apart. He shook the hand of each player as he brought them out and told them they were outstanding and he congratulated them for having perfect season. There was still ten minutes left in the game, but the Panthers bench didn't let anybody down. The second team carried on playing excellent basketball. The score at the end of the game was Ashland 79, Elkhart 51. Denny was the team leader with 27 points. As the game ended the home town fans gave the entire team another standing ovation and the fans and the team stood around together on the hardwood floor talking, laughing and enjoying the great game and celebrating their great season for the next 30 minutes.

The final game of the 1957 season was played on Friday, February 22, at Divernon. Jerry's sports column said, "Divernon came out with a fast start and jumped to an early lead. Divernon held the lead at the end of the first period 19 to 16. But the pace was too fast for Divernon and Ashland was just getting warmed up. Gary was really running out there handling the offense and passing the ball to the open man.

By the close of the first half, the Panthers had come from behind and were in the lead 50 to 38. Intense final play followed in the second half as the Panthers built their lead. When the third period ended the starters had scored 86 points. Then Coach Hoff put the reserves in to play and they carried on for the entire fourth period. The starting five Jerry, Gary, Denny, Donny and Jack watched their regular season end from the bench.

The final game score was 95 to 68. Denny finished strong again as the leading scorer with 29 points. Jack added 17, Donny 16, Jerry 15, and Gary had 9 points. Points were contributed from the bench as well, Glenn added 5, and Bob 2 and Wally 2 points, bringing the season closing score up to 95. Tournament play and March Madness was right around the corner."

In addition to being one of the best guards in the state, Jerry was becoming a fine sports reporter. His biggest dream in life was to become a famous sports announcer like Harry Carry up in Chicago. If anybody wanted to find Jerry Conner on a Saturday night or Sunday morning they could find him at Brownback's Drug Store where he worked as a soda jerk.

Also, there was an old café in Ashland on the square where Jerry, Gary, and the rest of the kids in high school would hang out when they had a chance. They had an old Seeburg jukebox and all the girls in town liked to go in there and dance. Way back then a fountain soda was only 10 cents and you could have a couple of squirts of flavoring added for free. Cherry, chocolate, or vanilla flavors in a soda were all the rage. In 1957 the vanilla that was used to flavor drinks contained 35% alcohol so if you could get a lot of vanilla mixed in your drink, and if you drank enough of them you might get a slight buzz. It was almost as good as a rum and coke, but not quite. Elvis songs and rock and roll were popular then, and girls whose parents wouldn't allow them to listen to that kind of music on the radio at home would come down to the café where they could play songs and dance. Parents then were still listening to the big bands like Glenn Miller.

As much as the Panthers enjoyed their perfect season, playing basketball was not over for them yet. They all were thinking they could go a long way in tournament play. None of the seniors Gary, Jerry, Jack, Denny and Wally, were ready to retire from high school basketball. Most assuredly Denny and Jack would be accepting college scholarships to play basketball, but Gary, Jerry, and Wally were not so sure of their future. None of the seniors could afford to go on to college without the aid of basketball scholarships.

During the next few weeks though, the Panthers were focusing their attention on winning their District

Tournament, and continuing on to the Regional Tournament and beyond. For the first week after their regular season ended they worked out everyday without any basketballs, and they really loved it.

They understood the importance of being in the best possible condition they could be in and they worked hard with Coach Hoff to get their bodies in shape. They wanted to be able to outrun anybody they might face in the tournament. They also wanted to have more endurance than any other team they would face. They knew without a doubt Coach Hoff's tough conditioning regimen had given them the edge they had needed to win several of their games. Somewhere in mid-December it had dawned on them. And they even began taking those awful horse pill vitamins the coach had been giving them. They looked forward to and enjoyed their workouts with Coach Hoff.

On Friday of the first week of training for the playoffs they had to run circles around the gym for half an hour. Jack was really tired and wanted to stop running and he asked the coach, "When are you going to let us rest coach?"

"When Glenn Savage sweats, then you can rest." Coach Hoff said. He said that because Glenn had a special medical condition that prevented him from sweating.

"Go splash some water on yourself." Jack said running by Glenn.

Then the coach told them to run the other direction for half an hour. After that they ran sprints for 15 minutes. At the end of the week Coach Hoff gave them all a present for playing perfect all season long. The coach gave them all new warm up suits that were deep purple with white trim and had a darker purple panther leaping across the chest and the word

"Panthers" written in large white script across the back. Everybody loved their new warm up suits.

During their second week of pre-tournament practices Coach Hoff had them work on the basic fundamentals of their game. They had practiced every defense and every set play on offense they were going to use in the tournament. At the end of their last practice before the District Tournament began everybody on the team was in the showers except Donny and Coach Hoff. Donny had waited until the very last moment to do his 100 daily free throws. And he was staying later to get them; Coach Hoff was helping him by getting the ball and passing it to him. So Donny didn't have to move away from the free throw line. They were chatting about baseball. Donny was telling the coach how much he really wanted to be a major league first baseman.

Now all the other guys on the team had shot their free throws during school hours on a pass to leave class and go to the gym. But, Donny loved school and didn't want to miss one minute of class time if he didn't have to. While Jerry and Gary were getting out of the shower they concocted the biggest prank that was ever played on anybody at Ashland High School.

The unbelievable season had gone so well that their confidence level and team spirit were soaring into uncharted altitudes. They wanted to play a prank on Donny who they thought was "the coach's pet," and because he was really starting to play great basketball; but, mostly because he was the only junior on the starting team and they just really enjoyed picking on him.

Donny was definitely getting a little swagger in his walk from all the success that he and the team were having. So after their normally grueling practice session on the floor Donny had stayed after and was shooting baskets and talking to the coach. Donny only needed 25 more baskets to reach his hundred for the day. He actually made 24 out of the next 25 he shot that night with the coach. It was really late when he went into the locker room for his shower. He thought something was wrong and it was unusually strange because everybody had gone home without saying goodbye. When Donny went into the locker room to get his shower, Coach Hoff went straight home. Donny was in the shower alone singing and washing his head. Donny was exuberant about making 24 out-of 25 free throws and wished some of his teammates were there so he could brag about his great achievement.

Earlier, when the guys finished their showers and dressed, they had discussed the plan. They all thought it was a swell idea. They all went outside to the parking lot and waited until Donny was in the shower. Jack had peeped in the window and saw him going into the shower. Then, when they thought the coast was clear, they went out to Donny's brand new Nash.

Now Donny's dad was a farmer and Donny had his driver's license since he was fifteen. At that age though, he was restricted to driving between the hours of 7 A.M. and 7 P.M. So at the time of the prank Donny had been driving for two years and he had his regular driver's license. While Donny was showering, Jerry opened the double doors that were in the center of the wall opposite of the bleachers. It was pitch dark out around their parking lot beside the school. There weren't any street lights nearby. The only light around was the glittering, sparkling glow coming from all the stars in the night sky.

The strictest rules of all of Coach Hoff's rules were meant to protect the gym floor. Nobody was allowed on that floor, at any time, for any reason, without the coach's written permission. The exception was the basketball players who were on the team. Occasionally Pete would let some kids play ball on the weekend, but that was it. Nobody else was allowed out on the floor for any reason. And those players who were on the team had to be dressed in their complete uniforms wearing official Converse All Star basketball shoes that were white with purple laces. They were the only ones allowed on that blond hardwood floor.

Donny's new purple and white Nash Rambler Metropolitan was a beautiful little car. It was a mini car. Jerry, Gary, Denny, Jack and the rest of the team opened the unlocked doors (nobody in Ashland at the time, ever locked any doors). That tiny little car was the apple of Donny's eye and he loved it dearly. It had side mirrors on the front fenders, and it had fender skirts on the rear wheels and mud flaps on all the wheels. And as well, it had one of the most important new luxury items, air conditioning.

Gary, who was trying hard to hold back his laughing and chuckling at the very idea of the plan all along, couldn't control his laughter any more, and he began laughing his ridiculous laugh. That happened while the whole team lifted the beautiful purple and white Nash as easy as if it was a marshmallow. They carried it into the gym and set it down on the center of the basketball court. It was inside the circle that was on the center of the hardwood floor. They gingerly put it down and ran outside laughing and closed the doors behind them. Gary's ridiculous laugh actually was so infectious that they all began to laugh uncontrollably for several minutes before they went home. Then Gary and Jerry walked away together headed for Gary's house.

When Donny came out to the parking lot he had no idea what had happened to his car, he thought it had been stolen. Bob McCarthy who was staying late that evening to check the equipment, turn off the lights and lock the gymnasium doors, was astounded when he found Donny's car on the center of the gym floor. Immediately he went after Donny who he had just seen leaving the locker room.

"Quick come back into the gym—you've got to see this." Bob yelled from the double doors at Donny who seemed bewildered in the parking lot.

Donny saw the car and both he and Bob started to laugh.

"Those rotten pranksters." Bob said.

"I love it." Donny said.

Donny had a great sense of humor. He was easy going and took everything in stride. Earlier that night while shooting free throws with the coach, Donny had figured out that he might want to become a coach. Bob opened the double doors and Donny drove his beautiful little purple and white Nash Rambler off the basketball court and went home to the farm. He laughed all the way home.

The entire next week in school when the guys on the team kept bugging him to tell them how in the world he found out where his car was, he'd just smile and say, "I have my ways." He never told anybody that Bob told him where his car was. Coach Hoff never found out that a car had been driven across his sacred basketball court's old blond hardwood floor either.

It was the first Friday evening in March, Jerry and Gary had just calmed down from laughing so hard it hurt because of their brilliant prank. They were walking from practice and were almost at Gary's house.

"Stop—stop laughing, I can't take it anymore." Jerry said.

"Oh it hurts so much." Gary said, grabbing his stomach.

"Never laugh uncontrollably on an empty stomach." Jerry said. And Gary nodded his approval.

"I wish I was as good at writing as you are. Those sports articles you write in the paper every week are great....I have to finish a paper for English class this weekend and I'm having trouble with it." Gary said.

"Let's go in and grab a sandwich at your house before Denny gets here, and I'll try and help you with your writing." Jerry said.

They went into Gary's and Gary made them both a ham sandwich with lettuce, mustard, a large bread and butter pickle from Aunt Snig and Uncle Pete's garden with a large glass of milk and Oreo cookies.

"I feel like my writing rages like a river. I'm okay when it's flowing in its banks, but my writing rears up, gets out of control and floods everywhere. Your sports articles are so darned good I wish I could write clearly like you do." Gary said smacking his sandwich.

"You have to know what you're writing about. It's easy for me because I know my subject. What are you writing about?" Jerry said and swallowed big gulps of milk, then wiped the white from his upper lip.

"We were supposed to ask a question and then discuss it." Gary said.

"What's your question?" Jerry asked.

"Why is it that the earth is constantly spinning at a high speed, but we can't tell that it's moving?" Gary said.

"Wow, that's a great question. You're a brain. I mean you're really smart." Jerry said biting into a pickle.

"Yeah right, but I don't have any discussion. I don't know what to write." Gary said pushing the last bite of ham sandwich into his mouth and licking mustard from his fingers.

"You can write what ever you want to from there. I'm doing an article right now for the yearbook. It's sort of a letter from Mars. It's set in the future and everybody in our graduating class is going to live there, and Gary you're going to become a star comedian." Jerry said.

And they began dunking their cookies in milk.

"I'll probably have to talk about gravity and Sir Isaac Newton." Gary said.

"You could talk about air, and basketball. Get your game into the paper, you know write the way you play ball." Jerry said.

"Oh I get you. Have fun with it." Gary said.

"Yeah be creative and enjoy it." Jerry said.

"You know what, sometimes I like to just sit around and read the dictionary." Gary said. And he really did, but when heard himself say it he thought it was funny, and began to laugh again and Jerry laughed with him.

Denny's car blasted—Ahoogah! Jerry and Gary ran out of the house, jumped into Denny's jalopy. "Hey lets go over and see if Donny's car is still in the gym." Jerry said.

After finding the gym empty they wondered how Donny found his car while they cruised around neighborhoods, the square, and were looking for their friends all evening.

Later that night, driving back towards Gary's house, Denny said, "Aren't those new warm up suits the coach gave us the greatest?"

"Oh yeah, and we don't have to give them back. We get to keep them!" Jerry said.

"I think it's great the way coach had them made for us with our full names printed in white letters across the panther on the front. I guess we'll always be Panthers." Gary said.

"We'll always be a team." Jerry said.

"We'll always be best friends." Denny said.

Gary climbed out of the jalopy. "I'm working all day tomorrow at the lumber yard." Gary said.

"As usual, I'll be up at the soda fountain all day tomorrow and Sunday Morning." Jerry said, as he climbed out of the jalopy.

"I'll come by Sunday afternoon." Denny said, and drove away.

"Hey Gary I've been thinking about joining the Navy after school. I mean I just have a feeling that nobody is going to offer us a scholarship." Jerry said.

"Just don't worry about it. Maybe we won't get scholarships. So what? If that happens, then I'll go with you in the Navy." Gary said.

"Wow, wouldn't that be great? We could see the world together." Jerry said.

"Yeah so don't worry about it. Let's focus on one thing, winning our basketball games. I know we have an opportunity to get to the Sweet Sixteen, and I know we can win. I can feel it in my heart." Gary said.

"I know we can too.... See ya later Alligator!" Jerry said, turning and walking toward his house.

"After a while Crocodile!" Gary said, and ran into his house.

Chapter 11

Few schools in Illinois were as small as Ashland. They had the smallest senior class in 1957. Including Gary Pearn, there were nineteen students scheduled for graduation, seven girls and twelve boys. There would have been twenty kids in the class, but Helen Orne fell in love and dropped out of school.

Helen Orne was in the "Class of 1957." Or she should have been. Helen lived on a farm in the country between Ashland and Virginia. Her high school sweetheart was Richard Petefish who also, lived on a farm in the country toward Alexander. Helen eloped with Richard when she was only a sophomore. The young lovers were gone for two days and because nobody knew where they went, they were the talk of the town. Their parents were furious and wanted to have their marriage annulled when they came back. They didn't annul their marriage though, and the high school sweethearts settled down living in the country near Ashland and enjoyed an early start in life.

Back in those days, the smaller schools in the state had to play each other in District Tournaments. Each District hosted eight teams from small schools in their area. The team that won all three games in their District won their District Championship Trophy and went on to play in the Regional Tournament.

Larger schools entered the Illinois playoffs at their Regional Tournament. Schools from larger cities like Quincy, and Lanphier from Springfield, or Elm City would play their first games in the Regional Tournament. Smaller schools had an unfair disadvantage because they had to have three wins under their belt before they could compete in the Regional Tournaments. Most of the smaller schools in the state never went to their Regional Tournament's because they were always eliminated by stronger teams in their District Tournament competition.

Large schools started their tournament play in the Regionals just because they were big. What that meant was, in 1957 a small school had to win twelve games in a row to be crowned the State Champion. Large schools that began playing in the Regionals only had to win nine games in a row to be crowned the state champion. As difficult as it was to go from Regionals to become the State Champion, it was nearly an insurmountable task to go from being the District Tournament Champion to become the State Champion.

In the entire history of basketball in the State of Illinois if a small school somehow managed to win District (three games), Regional (three games), Sectional (two games), and make it into the "Sweet Sixteen," (four more games), then they were always eliminated by a bigger school in the first round of the "Sweet Sixteen." Nobody from a small school coming from a District Tournament had ever made it to the final eight teams in the history of the state playoffs.

Ashland had confident aspirations, and high hopes. Ashland thought they had a chance to do what no other small school had ever before accomplished. They thought they could make it into the "Sweet Sixteen," go beyond and win the State Championship. The "Sweet Sixteen" games were played at Champaign, in the gym at the University of Illinois, and the games were broadcast statewide on TV.

The 1957 District Tournament for Ashland was played on the Easton Hawks home court. Ashland played Tallula in their opening game. Tallula wore yellow uniforms that Bob McCarthy thought were the ugliest color for a team to wear. No matter what color they wore they posed no threat to the Panthers. The last time the two teams had met was at Ashland in the first game of the season. Throughout their season the Panthers had steadily grown and improved as a basketball team. Tallula couldn't have beaten the Panthers the first time they met, and there was literally nothing they could have done to win the second time either. Ashland won the game and had it well in hand all the way with a final score of 82 to 58. Denny was the leading scorer of the game with 23 points, but all five starters scored in double figures. Their scoring potential and ability to score from anywhere created a huge defensive problem for most of the teams they would face in tournament play.

If the Panthers continued to win then they continued to play. The loser was eliminated and their season was over when they were knocked out of the tournament. The winner of Ashland's District Tournament at Easton would go next to play in the Havana Regional on Havana's home court. The winner from the Havana Regional would continue to the Sectional. The winner of the sectional would then be in the "Sweet Sixteen" at the U. of I. That was the only path the Panthers could take in 1957 to get to play in the final state championship game.

All the players on the Panthers 1957 team loved playing basketball. They were outstanding athletes who really enjoyed excellent competition. They wanted an opportunity to play some of the great teams in the state like Collinsville, La Grange, Westinghouse and

Herrin. They wanted to meet another team that could keep up with them in their run and gun style of offense. They wanted to play another fast, high scoring team because they thought they just might be able to beat anyone.

The tougher the games were the harder Gary and the rest of the team played. They seemed able to play at the same level as any opponent they met, and then turn it up a notch, turn on the steam, and run away with a victory. If a team challenged them and actually played ball with them in their fast-paced run and gun style, then they would look them right in the eye, and play harder—they knew they could beat them. Four of their starters were seniors. If they lost, their high school careers were over. The door was slammed shut and that part of their life became history. None of the Panthers wanted that to happen.

Since the Panthers had beaten Tallula, they continued to play. They had to travel by bus to each game and they went back to the Easton Hawk's home court for their second night in a row. Their next opponent was Balyki. Earlier in the season they had embarrassed Balyki in front of their own fans on Balyki's home court with a score of 48 to 24. So Balyki knew who they were up against and they were out for revenge.

In the semifinal game against Balyki the Panthers struggled. In fact, they played poorly because they were a much better team than Balyki. But Balyki brought their best game of the entire season onto the floor that night, and the Panthers were trailing them for most of the game. They led Ashland in the first period 12 to 6, at the half Balyki led 26 to 12, and by the end of the third period they were continuing their lead. It seriously looked as if the Panthers were going to be eliminated.

At the beginning of the fourth period the Panthers came back strong with good shooting and powerful rebounding. With plenty of drive and power in the fourth period, the Panthers came from behind to take the lead. The strength of their conditioning program enabled them to consistently increase their game intensity in the final minutes. Balyki seemed to be wilting and running out of steam as the Panthers turned the steam on. Their endurance level was astronomical. The final score was Ashland 57, Balyki 50. Balyki had played their best game of the season and given the Panthers more than they could handle for three periods. Balyki had played a very respectable game. The Panthers shook hands with them after the game and told them they played well because nobody had been able to stay in front of them for three periods all season long. Jack was the leading scorer for Ashland with 16 points and was tied for high scoring honors with Ebken from Balyki who also had scored 16 points. The Panthers were still alive and would continue to play in the tournament. They would make the long bus ride tomorrow for the third night in a row and return to Easton. The winner of tomorrow's game would be the District Champion and go on to Havana to participate in the Regional Tournament.

It was déjà vu for Ashland. The opponent was the Easton Hawks on their home floor. Their home fans always raised a deafening cheer in their gym. In the 1956 District Championship game Easton had won 66 to 60, and had ended the Panthers season with bitter disappointment. This was the game that hundreds of Hawk's fans were waiting for because the Hawks suffered only one loss to Ashland in the 1957 season and they wanted retribution. They wanted to blow Ashland off the court and send them packing back home finished for the season. Going into this game if the Hawks could win it, they would give the Panthers their only loss, but the Hawks would play on and go to Havana.

The biggest difference in this game was the fact that Ashland had given Easton their only loss of the 1957 season. Coach Hoff gave the Panthers this sage advice before they loaded the bus for the third night in a row to go to the game. "Play this game. Forget your past games with the Hawks and play this game. Give it everything you have. Forget their cheering fans. Focus on what you do best and do it on the court tonight. I know we can go up there and WIN this game."

If Ashland did win, of course it would end the Hawks season. It meant the Hawks would suffer their second loss of the year, by the hands of the Panthers, in games played both at home and away. The main difference between the two teams was one player. Both teams had the same old coaches and the same old guys on their teams. Gary Pearn was the main difference between the 1956 season and the 1957 season. Gary made the Ashland Panthers a better basketball team.

The Panthers had acquired a premier starting guard. Gary's ball handling skills, quickness, game knowledge and his, "never say die," attitude had elevated the Panthers to new levels of play. Gary seemed to grow in confidence with each game he played with the Panthers. He was spinning, passing, shooting and creating new moves in every game. His friends and teammates appreciated what skill and talent he brought onto the court for their team. They knew when he had the ball something magical was about to happen. When Gary had the ball they were always alert and waiting to see what he would do. In the blink of an eye Gary could pass the ball to them. In a heartbeat Gary could release a forty foot jump shot that would rip the net with a loud swoosh.

Everybody likes a winner. Gary and Jerry ran the offense and made the full court zone press defense click. Gary's speed, confidence and sense of humor had helped the whole team grow better. When they went to Easton to play the Hawks for the second time, it was their best game of the 1957 season.

Two extra fan buses trailed them over the miles toward Easton that night, and many other fans drove up from the Ashland community to support them. The Cheerleaders had their bus filled to capacity with AHS students, and they sang and cheered all the way up to Easton. So that night, four buses left Ashland in line followed by nearly fifty cars. Charlie Forman the scorekeeper, Blondie Field the timer, (and Donny's dad) and Pete Gutmann the school custodian, all went to the game.

There were almost as many fans from Ashland as there were fans from Easton at the game that night. The game proved to be a thriller. The first period was lightning quick as both teams ran equally well together. At the conclusion of the first period the score was tied 16 to 16. In the second period Gary proved to be the fastest player on the floor. The Hawks were playing tough on defense, so instead of trying to force a pass, Gary began driving the ball, dribbling through cracks in their defense and making beautiful no look finger-tip lay-ups. At the half the score was Panthers 37, Hawks 21.

The Easton Hawks presented the toughest competition the Panthers faced all year. They had beaten every opponent except Ashland by 20 to 30 points. Their average winning score was 25 points or better. Since their only loss was at the hands of the Panthers they were playing for revenge.

Gary could shoot from anywhere; he was an excellent shooter. When alone and unguarded he could swish fifteen footers all night long. His superior speed was what was so impressive, especially in the way he drove through the defense to make lay-ups. Gary would either make a lay-up, or draw a foul from the Hawk center that would step up to try and block his shot. Then Gary made all of his foul shots. Or Gary would do a little bobble-de-boop with his head, drive around a Hawk in a flash and pull up for his beautiful left-handed jump shot. Either way Gary was scoring.

In the middle of the fourth period the Easton starting center fouled out trying to block one of Gary's lay-ups. By the score of 83 to 67 Ashland won their first District Championship Trophy. The Panther's trounced the Hawks on their home floor by 16 points.

How good were the Easton Hawks? Well they had beaten Havana in the regular season by 30 points. Now the Panthers would be the first team in the history of their school to play in their Regional Tournament. Ashland had made it; they were going to play on; they would soon be traveling to Havana to compete for their Regional Trophy.

On the way home everybody from Ashland was really celebrating. Bob McCarthy had the Trophy in the seat next to him and he was protecting it like it was a newborn baby. What a grand good feeling that

Championship victory was for the team, the school, and the whole community. That night people in town were celebrating into the wee hours of the night. The tiny little sleepy community of Ashland, Illinois had woken up.

The game was highly touted and followed avidly by basketball fans all across central Illinois. It was listened to on the radio with special interest by those teams that were beginning their tournament play in Havana and might have to face the Ashland Panthers in the playoff.

Ernie Hoff was in his third year of coaching at Ashland and he had never felt more proud of his team. They had 28 wins, no losses and were bringing home Ashland's first District Tournament Trophy.

For Gary who had transferred from Elm City, leaving his mother, sisters, and little brother to reach his goal and become a starting point guard on a Varsity team, the Ashland Panther's season was a dream that came true! Gary had been the top gun in the game scoring 25 points. Denny made 22 points, and Jack made 19. Jerry made 9 points and Donny contributed 8. The starting five had played the whole game. Those five guys were and would always be basketball stars.

"When the going gets tough, the tough get going." Coach said,

at practice Monday afternoon. The Panthers had won three basketball games, three nights in a row on Thursday, Friday and Saturday. Monday and Tuesday would be light workout days for the team. They would rest on Wednesday and, if all went well, play three more basketball games on Thursday, Friday and Saturday.

Mostly the Panthers practiced zone defense and Coach Hoff talked a lot trying to get the team mentally prepared for the Regional Tournament. Coach Hoff was from Havana. His parents lived there and he had played basketball four years as a starting guard for the Havana Ducks team. He knew their coach well and knew what tricks he had up his sleeve.

In order to make it all the way through the tournament and be competitive Coach Hoff told the Panthers that the second team was going to have to step up and be ready to play. It was possible they could be facing the Havana Ducks on their home floor in the second game. That could happen if Ashland won their first game and Havana also won their first game.

If they had to face the Ducks in all probability the winner of the second game would face Lanphier, a very big team from Springfield. Ashland had never played Lanphier before and they were excited about the possibility of beating them. Coach Hoff told the team that the Easton Hawks had beaten the Havana Ducks by 30 points in the regular season on the Ducks home floor. It really was no news to the Panthers because they read the papers and were well aware of what other teams were doing.

"If we play Havana in the second game, then I'm going to start the second team. I know we can beat the Ducks. They like to play a slow passing old fashion style of ball. They walk, walk, walk—they put teams to sleep. They get fast teams out of their rhythm, out of their game and make them play at a slow rate. They rarely ever score more than 50 points in a game. The second team will play the whole game. The first team will be on the bench if we need them. The Ducks will pass the ball ten to fifteen times before they shoot." Coach Hoff said.

He made Bob, Glenn and Wally practice baseball passes for 30 minutes on Monday and Tuesday. They would practice while the other players ran sprints up the floor. Wally would throw the ball all the way down court to Bob or Glenn at the free throw line. But each throw had to be perfectly timed to beat the Panthers down court while they were running as fast as they could. Who ever caught the pass would then make an easy undefended shot before the team ran down the floor. Then they would turn around and do it at the other end with Bob passing to Glenn and Wally, or Glenn passing to Bob and Wally, while everybody else ran their sprints.

In the game against the Ducks, Coach Hoff planned to unveil his new second team shotgun offense. He wanted to be able to score as quickly as possible. If the Ducks walked down the floor and passed the ball ten or fifteen times and then made two points, Wally would take the ball out and immediately make a baseball pass the length of the court to the free throw line. Bob or Glenn would take off toward the free throw line as soon as the Ducks shot the ball.

If Bob caught the ball at the free throw line all alone he would then go in for an easy lay-up, or make a high percentage undefended two points. The idea was to do it more quickly than the Ducks could run back and get set in their zone defense. If they missed the basket, (and eventually they would) there was a rebound. When the Panthers got the rebound they would immediately throw the baseball pass down court to the free throw line. Bob or Glenn would catch the ball and put it in the basket. That was the offensive strategy for the game, if they had to play the Havana

Ducks. Putting the second team in would give the starting team a night off and they could rest and be ready to play Lanphier Saturday night. They wanted to be ready to play their best against Lanphier.

The Panthers also practiced three or four set plays that depended on what Gary did with the ball. If he dribbled the ball left, right, straight, or passed, then everybody knew what play to go into. Gary's specialty came at the top of the key when he pulled up and shot a left handed jump shot. In 1957 those were two point shots. All those shots Gary made from the top of the key, by current basketball rules are three point baskets. If Gary dribbled toward Donny, playing in the forward position, at that moment in time Donny would set a screen for Gary's defender. Donny always called it "the old screen and roll," Gary would dribble around the screen, and then Donny would turn and break toward the basket. Then Gary would have three options: he could pass the ball to Donny for a short shot or a lay-up; he could continue dribbling into the corner and either shoot or pass the ball back out front to Jerry; or if nobody bothered to guard him, then he would make a short quick jump shot for two points. Gary and Donny played well together on the left. They were both left handed. Jerry and Denny also play well together on the right, and they were both right handed. They were a perfectly tuned, well matched set of basketball players. When you added their fiercely competitive center Jack Lynn, then the 1957 Panthers were a perfect team.

Chapter 12

Gary and Jerry were best friends and they talked basketball, and they talked often, it was always about how to play the game right and get approval from their coach, about how they were always trying to be sure they didn't let their teammates down, about how they were trying not to fail, and trying to succeed, and implicit in all of their talks was how they were motivated by trying to make their parents and friends proud of them. Most significantly was how they were always trying to prove to themselves that they were worthy and could make it on the basketball court and thus in life.

Basketball simply was what life was all about in a small town in Illinois during the 1950s. The Panthers had a chance to do something significant and they wanted to do their very best. Gary's mom—Dee worked at the Elm City Café. She was enthusiastically and passionately proud of Gary's success in basketball. She was busily slicing fresh homemade banana cream pies and putting them in the counter display case when a regular customer at the restaurant talked to her about how well her son Gary was doing playing ball in Ashland. Nothing could have made her feel more proud.

"I'm praying for him... Floyd Sorrells, the owner of the Café told me if Gary's team makes it to the finals over in Champaign, he's going to close the restaurant and drive me and his family over to watch Gary and his team play!" Dee said, refilling the customer's coffee cup.

"I've listened to every one of his games when they've been on radio. I think Gary is a great ball player." The customer said.

Lanphier a much bigger school was rated number one in the Havana Regional Tournament. Ashland was rated second in the tournament, and their first game was scheduled against Athens. This was what Jerry wrote in his sports column about the game, "The Panthers took an early lead and held it the whole game. The Panthers outscored Athens in every period. In the first period the score was 19 to 13; but, by the half the score was 39 to 25. The Panthers continued to play well as Athens made a run in the third period but were unsuccessful. The final score was 76 to 63. Three seniors were tied for the high score: Gary, Denny and Jack all scored 20 points. The Ashland Panthers set the school record when they won their 28th and 29th games, the most wins in a season ever recorded by the purple and white."

The win gave the Panthers a chance to play The Havana Ducks who had also won their first game. If they could beat the Ducks, then most likely they would face Lanphier in the Championship game because Lanphier had won their game easily. Ashland was impressed by the size of Lanphier's band; they had 105 kids playing instruments. Their band was larger than the sum total of all the kids that went to Ashland High School. The Lanphier cheerleaders were equally impressive with 21 kids, more students than were in Ashland's entire senior class of 19 kids. From that point on, after talking it over with Mr. Bierman, Coach Hoff arranged to bring the Ashland School and Alumni band to every tournament game. In addition, he also got approval to bring the Junior Varsity Cheerleaders: Carol Gerdes, Lynell Field and Elizabeth

Wright. So they would at least have eight cheerleaders on the floor at the games cheering the Panthers on to victory.

Nobody in the state truly thought the Ducks posed any threat to the Panthers. Looking at the records Ashland was 29 and 0 for the season. The Ducks were an average team that had lost to Easton by 30 points. They just didn't play well, or match up very well against fast-break run and gun offenses.

Occasionally a coach can implement a game winning strategy that will surprise everybody, and tonight Coach Hoff was going to unveil his new strategy. Red Van Etten, the coach for the Ducks also had a game strategy. Red's plan was for the Ducks to get the lead early and hold onto the ball. He knew Ashland would win if they allowed the Panthers to get rolling in their fast-break.

In the locker room before the game, Red said, "Try and get the lead early. Then hold onto the ball until you see an easy basket. Shoot only when you know for sure you can make it. Walk when you are playing offense. We don't want to try and run with these guys. Keep the score real low and we might win."

The Ducks came out of their locker room wearing their maroon school colors; they were fired up and ready to play basketball. The second team for Ashland took the floor: Wally, Bob, Glenn, Edgar and Graham. The Ducks easily won the tip-off that went to one of their forwards, but when he missed his first shot Bob snagged the rebound, tossed a quick baseball pass down to Wally who made an easy lay-up. The next time up the floor the Ducks passed the ball around about a dozen times, but they missed an easy shot and Glenn came up with the rebound. Glenn threw the ball down to Wally who got his second easy lay-up and the Panthers were leading early 4 to 0.

Coach Red Van Etten was particularly nervous and he paced up and down on the sidelines. Ashland had the lead and he couldn't do anything about it. Once Ashland had the lead they controlled the game. The Panthers could score like lightning, and then the ducks would bring the ball in bounds and leisurely walk around passing the ball as if they had all day. They walked everywhere they dribbled and didn't run one step on offense all night long. They were walking around as if their feet were stuck in molasses.

When the Ducks brought the ball in they simply walked past the half court line then stood around on the periphery of the Panthers 2-3 zone defense passing the ball around. They never really attacked the Panthers defense. There weren't any shot clocks to limit the amount of time a team could hold onto the basketball, so the Ducks held onto the ball for two or three minutes every time they were on offense. The Ducks slowed the pace of the game down trying to put the Panthers to sleep so they could catch them off guard and make easy baskets. The strategy didn't work though. The second team had only played in one other entire game all year. They had beaten Farmersville.

The Panthers second team was not experienced enough to have developed a game rhythm. The Ducks couldn't lull them and get them out of rhythm because they didn't have any. They were so excited to be starting and out on the floor playing ball that literally nothing would have dampened their spirits. The shotgun fast-break the Panthers had unveiled really frustrated the Ducks. The Panthers scored most of their baskets before the Ducks could even waddle down court and get set in their zone defense. At half time the Panthers were leading 44 to 20. The Panthers had the game well in hand and Ashland's fans were exuberant. The Havana Ducks' large crowds of fans were stunned and sat there watching silently most of the night.

Coach Red Van Etten was acting nervous and not really doing a very good job of coaching. His Ducks had problems with fast-break teams all season long. Also, the Ashland team had athletes that were in much better physical condition than his team. They couldn't foul the Ashland players either because the Panthers were excellent free throw shooters.

In the third period Ashland gained nine more points in the lead as the Ducks continued to walk on offense. The score was 60 to 27. In the fourth period, just so the second team could get more experience, Coach Hoff told the Panthers to run the full court zone press defense. The woeful Ducks just couldn't fly; they never scored another basket. In the end, the game was a blow out, Ashland 83, Havana 27. Wally was the high scorer for the game with 23 points. Glenn made 19 and Bob made 18 points. Edgar put in 14, and Graham contributed 9 points. It was the Panthers 30th win. They couldn't wait to play Lanphier.

The Purple Panther mascot danced around on the floor with all eight of Ashland's cheerleaders at the beginning of the Regional Championship game. Ashland's band that was made of current students and alumni played the school fight song as the Panthers came onto the floor to warm up. David Winklemann, a senior, was the school mascot.

Lanphier had their mascot, a Lion, a senior girl. The two mascots played around during the game and after the game they became good friends.

Lanphier's great team wore orange with black trim. They were all good athletes and the game seemed evenly matched as the first period ended tied 24 to 24. The second period was nip and tuck, as the score was tied 46 to 46 at the half. After about a minute into the second half Coach Hoff pulled Jerry out and put Wally into the game. Wally played both guard and forward with equal proficiency and he was usually the man Coach Hoff went to in a game to come off the bench cold, make a jump shot or two, and spark the team. Wally scored the first four points of the second half, and Ashland never looked back. After two minutes Coach Hoff put Jerry back into the game, but by then Wally had helped his team turn on the steam. The score at the end of the third period was 79 to 61.

At the beginning of the fourth period Lanphier had the ball, but Gary stole it away and made a long baseball pass to Jerry who took it in for an easy lay-up. It happened so fast Lanphier didn't know what hit them, then as they brought the ball back up the court, Gary and Jerry switched defensive sides so that Gary could get at the man with the ball. Lightning struck twice when Gary scooped the ball out, with his right hand and threw another full court pass to Jerry. Jerry caught the ball chest high and with a single graceful stride made a very easy lay-up and the score was 83 to 61.

Lanphier never gave up and continued to play hard, but they looked like a race horse that had given everything it had at the first of half of the race and would struggle in to the finish line ten lengths behind the winner. The score was 103 to 85. In the final two minutes Coach Hoff pulled the entire first team off the court. Coach Hoff said, "After they score again hold the ball and pass it around for the final minute." At the end of the game the exuberant Ashland fans ran onto the floor surrounding the Panthers celebrating wildly the Panthers overwhelming victory over Lanphier. The final score was 103 to 87. Jack and Gary had tied for high score with 25 points. Denny made 23, and Donny and Jerry had tied with 13 points and Wally had contributed 4 points from the bench. The Panthers had made that win look easy. After the game the Coach for the Lanphier Lions shook hands with Coach Hoff and said, "Good luck, you've got a great ball team. I hope you make it all the way—you're that good."

Gary and Jack went to the center court to accept the 1957 Regional Championship Trophy for Ashland High School. They both wiped tears from their eyes, tears of joy, as they listened to the award being presented. The presenter said, "The Ashland Panthers have broken all of their school records winning 31 games with no losses this year. These ten young men are the best team to ever play basketball at Ashland. The trophy reads, The 1957 Havana Regional Tournament First Place; congratulations Panthers, you deserve it. This is the fifth first place trophy the Panthers have won this year. Next Friday the Panthers will represent our region at the Sectional Tournament in Springfield, good luck in the tournament, we'll be rooting for you to go all the way!"

Gary and Jack lifted the trophy high over their heads. It was a night they would never forget and they celebrated on their buses all the way back home. It was the greatest feeling to win the Havana Regional the players had ever known. On the way home Coach Hoff told the team, "The way you won this tournament was exceptional. When you beat my old team the Ducks, I felt like a great weight had been lifted off my shoulders. I love you guys. When we get home we're going to have to start building a new trophy case to hold all of the new trophies."

Four teams were in the Sectional Tournament in Springfield: Ashland, Elm City, Springfield and Waverly. On Friday night Elm City and Waverly would play first, and then Ashland and Springfield would play. Incredibly Ashland had beaten Easton in the District Tournament and Havana in the Regional Tournament, on their home floor in front of all their fans. Now they had to face Springfield on their home floor in front of all their cheering fans. The Panthers took it in stride. They were not worried about who or where they were playing. They were thankful to be in the tournament and just wanted to bring their best game to their challenging opponent. The four teams were all excellent teams with outstanding regular seasons, but the Panthers were the undefeated team. All four teams had won their own Regional Tournament. Ashland had the best record, but they were ranked third, behind Elm City who was second, and Springfield was first. Odds were against them because they were from such a small community.

Ashland came into Springfield, their State Capitol, and a city of nearly 200,000 inhabitants, ready to play. They had good workouts with Coach Hoff on Monday, Tuesday and Wednesday, and then rested until Friday night's 7:00 P.M. game time. It was the first time Ashland had traveled to Springfield to play basketball.

Although nearly everybody from Ashland was at the game to cheer the Panthers on, the gymnasium seated around 11,000 people most of whom were wearing red and cheering for Springfield. The Ashland fans cheered loudly though as their Student and Alumni Band played the school fight song and the Panthers ran out onto the floor for warm ups.

Earlier that evening Elm City had easily handled their game with Waverly. The Elm City Cougars started fast and were leading after the first period 16 to 9. At the half they had built their lead to 34 to 18. At the beginning of the third period Waverly made a run, but never got closer than within 7 points of the Cougars. At the end of the third period the score was 60 to 53. They continued to battle basket for basket in the fourth period, but Waverly couldn't manage to come from behind losing 72 to 65. Ronny Jay was the high scorer with 23 points.

Ronny Jay and Coach Quinn were hoping Ashland would beat Springfield. They wanted to beat the Panthers in the Sectional Championship game. Ronny thought Gary would be an easy push-over for him, and he thought he could give Gary trouble all over the court. After all, Ronny had been the starting point guard for Elm City four years in a row and in his senior year he had been voted the team Captain.

Ronny Jay usually led his team in scoring, mostly because he'd rather shoot than pass, but he was a dirty player on defense and tried to get away with murder when the referees were not watching him. During the season he had elbowed ribcages, punched unsuspecting players, poked fingers into other player's eyes, and ears, pushed players in the back, and he had tripped players while they were running up the court. Other than those few bad qualities, Ronny was a pretty fine ball player.

Coach Quinn really wanted Elm City to defeat Ashland. He thought that Ashland really hadn't beaten any good teams from the better schools. He thought the win against Lanphier was just a fluke and that if they played Lanphier nine more times, Lanphier would win every game. He had a very physical game plan in mind for Ashland if they met in the final game. Coach Quinn hated Gary and generally disliked the other players on Gary's team who were poor and from a tiny farming community. He thought they were all a bunch of redneck, hicks and backwards hillbillies. He hated Gary and everybody like him that came from broken families. Next to poverty, Coach Quinn thought that divorce was the most evil social ill in the nation. He was looking forward to attacking the Panthers and he wanted to end their string of undefeated games. Coach Quinn was a cold, cruel and heartless man.

Springfield High School came onto their home floor and the noise in the gymnasium was deafening. Their band played and the crowd cheered wildly for Springfield High. They were dressed in their colorful away uniforms giving up the home floor uniform to Ashland, but that wasn't any real advantage. Springfield wore red and black with white trim. The Panthers wore their white home uniforms with purple trim. Nobody had beaten the Panthers in their home uniforms or on their own home floor for over two years.

Jerry Conner in his next sports column said, "Ashland hushed a rambunctious crowd of nearly 11,000 fans early after Jack tipped the ball to Denny who ripped a long jumper for the first points in the game. Next Gary scooped the ball away from Springfield's point guard and dribbled down to set the offense. After a set pick and roll Gary passed the ball to Donny who made a ragged hook shot and Ashland took the early lead 4 to 0. The first period ended with a score of 21 to 15.

In the second period Springfield fought back and filled the crowd with excitement when they took the lead. They couldn't hold the lead as the Panthers turned on the steam and the lead seesawed back and forth, but at the half Ashland held the lead 44 to 41.

In the third period Ashland opened up their full court press zone defense and began to shred Springfield's offense. After three minutes Coach Hoff put Wally, Glenn and Bob into the game in place of Jerry, Gary and Donny. Then Ashland dropped into their intimidating 3-2 half court zone with Jack out front. Ashland stayed in that zone for the next five minutes. Then Jerry, Gary and Donny came back into the game. As the period ended the score was 67 to 61.

In the fourth period Jack and Denny were playing with four fouls, but the Springfield center and one of their forwards fouled out. The depth of the Springfield bench was excellent. When two players from Springfield entered the game with fresh legs Springfield began to play better. In the final seconds Springfield tied the score at 88 forcing a five minute overtime.

In the overtime Jack again tipped the ball to Denny who ripped another long jumper. When Springfield's center missed a shot Donny grabbed the rebound and passed it to Jerry. Jerry passed the ball to Jack who scored two points. Immediately after that Gary made an excellent steal, as Springfield tried to bring the ball up the court, and he made an easy lay-up. With the overtime score 94 to 88, Coach Hoff gave the signal for the Panthers to hold the ball.

When Ashland began holding the ball, Springfield came out and began to foul aggressively. Coach Hoff called a timeout. He put Wally, Bob, Glenn and Edgar into the game and moved Donny up to play center. 'Hold the ball until the final few seconds, and then pass it to Donny. Donny you make your final shot.' At the end Bob passed the ball to Donny who was standing up at the free throw line. Donny dribbled once and went up for an awkward looking hook shot that he released before the final buzzer. Donny's hook shot bounced off the rim onto the backboard rolled around the cylinder three times and spun into the net. The final score was 101 to 92. Denny was the high scorer with 27 points. Jack made 23 and Gary made 22 points. Donny made 13 and Jerry made 12 points. Bob contributed 4 points at the free throw line.

The victory was Ashland's 32nd win of the season. Ashland will play Elm City for the Sectional Championship. This is a match up that Gary, Jack and Denny have been waiting for all season for private reasons. Everybody should come out and cheer the Panthers on. Another win will send Ashland to Champaign for the 'Sweet Sixteen' for the first time in the history of the school." It was the longest column Jerry had ever published.

On the bus ride back to Ashland Jack, Gary and Jerry sat together discussing a strategy for the coming game. They were well aware of the bias of Elm City's Coach Quinn, and of the conflicts caused by Ronny

Jay. They were plotting together to show Ronny Jay and Coach Quinn that they were the better team and that individually they were the better athletes. Their main plan was to play the best basketball they had ever played. "Get the ball to me, the Elm City Cougars center cannot block my shots. Get the ball to me and we'll beat them good." Jack said.

Gary and Jerry agreed that at every opportunity they would forget their regular set plays and throw lightning quick passes up to Jack all night long. On the bus they celebrated their 32nd win, but all the Panthers went home straight to bed to get enough rest to play aggressively in the Sectional Championship game. Jack dropped Jerry and Gary off at Gary's house and drove away. Jerry said, "I know we can win tomorrow and make it into the 'Sweet Sixteen'."

"Let's show them what we're made of and play with integrity. I want to shake their hands, and see the look on their faces after we win." Gary said.

Chapter 13

On Saturday night the Ashland Panthers took the floor in the gymnasium at Springfield High School. They were ready to play the Elm City Cougars for the Sectional Championship. Earlier in the locker room Coach Quinn had told the team his game strategy. He wanted them to play a tough rough and tumble physical game. He was putting his second team forwards in as starters. Coach Quinn said, "Foul their forwards especially that Bast kid. I want him out of the game. Foul their center too. Don't worry about fouling out because I'll have the starting forwards come in and replace you."

"What about Pearn?" Ronny Jay asked.

"Play him rough, but don't foul out. We need you in there to handle the ball and make points." Coach Quinn said.

The Cougars took the floor in their bright crimson uniforms. Gary lined up around the outer circle at center court right beside Ronny Jay. Ronny Jay looked at Gary with a sneering smile. Gary had a plan in mind. He knew sometimes if players were angry or lost their temper it could have a negative affect on their game. Gary had decided he might get Ronny Jay to lose his temper in the game. As everybody lined up around the circle waiting for the referee to toss the ball in the air for tip-off, Gary crouched like a panther getting ready to pounce on a victim.

Now Ronny Jay was a pretty big guy and he was a year older than any other player on the floor that night. Also, almost gorilla like thick hair covered his arms and legs. As the referee began to raise his arm to toss the ball Gary reached his hand out to Ronny Jay's furry leg, grabbed a handful of hair and ripped it out by the roots, just as Jack leaped up to tip the ball. Ronny Jay let out a shriek in pain, but nobody noticed because everybody was watching the ball. That had done the trick though, Ronny Jay's temper exploded and he was fighting mad. He played the whole game boiling in anger, furiously trying to push, bump and trip Gary.

Jack won the tip-off jump and pushed the ball toward Gary. In a flash Gary made a lay-up and Ashland took the early lead. Gary knew and loved all the guys on the Elm City team with the exception of Ronny. These were the guys Gary had played with a year ago on the JV. They had suffered only one loss when Gary was their point guard and it was to the team he was now playing on, the Ashland Panthers. In the first period Ronny Jay was called three times for fouling Gary. Gary made all six of his free throw shots.

Every time Gary had the ball on offense he'd throw a quick no look pass to Jack. Every time Jerry had the ball on offense he'd throw a quick no look pass to Jack. In the first period Jack made four free throws. Every time Gary or Jerry passed the ball to Jack he made points. In the first period Jack made every shot he took. The Panthers were beginning to roll over the Cougars. Gary made a couple of beautiful 40 foot left handed jumpers that hit nothing but net. The first period ended with the score Ashland 20, Elm City 13. But the Panthers were just getting warmed up.

During the break Ronny Jay was in a snit. Coach Quinn was livid. Coach Quinn had never really watched Gary play ball before; for three years in Elm City he had ignored him. The thought of it enraged him. Gary had performed magnificently in the first period. Coach Quinn finally began to see what a great player Gary was.

Gary played exceptionally well, handling the ball with ease. He helped spark the fast break in the second period. With unselfish and amazingly quick passes Gary continued to feed the ball in to Jack. Coach Quinn's strategy began to seriously backfire because several times after Gary threw a blazing pass to Jack who would make a basket, Denny or Donny would get fouled and make both of their free throw shots. Ashland had three unanswered four point plays back-to-back-to-back.

But Jack was in his sweet spot all night long and he called for the ball every time Gary set the offense. At half time Ronny Jay had three fouls and he was fuming. Three other Cougars had four fouls. Denny, and Donny who had been punched, pushed, kicked and tripped all night were bruised, but not angry. Having a coach who was once a Marine had taught them to keep cool and be level headed. But every time they had been knocked down by a Cougar they picked themselves up and gave the business right back to the guy who had fouled them. Sometimes they hit back harder than they had been hit. The Panthers were a very tough well conditioned group of strong farm boys. Not one of them would walk away from a fight. So by the half time break Denny and Donny both had four fouls. The amazing thing was the score Ashland 64, Elm City 23. It was not even close.

At half time Coach Hoff said, "Boys it looks like we're in a real dog fight out there. Try not to get killed. We still have four more games after this as long as we keep winning. Bob gave me his clip board with a red circle around points scored in the half by Jack. Jack has made 9 two point shots for 18 points and 7 free throws for a total of 25 points in the first half. His shooting percentage is 92%. Jack is blazing a trail to the record for highest points in one game. Let's help him. I want everybody on the floor to keep feeding the ball to Jack." Jerry, Gary and Jack looked at each other and broke out laughing.

It was a rather unusual game because both of the Panthers starting forwards fouled out. But the first player to leave the game was Ronny Jay. Just as soon as Gary had the ball in his hands in the second half Ronny Jay tripped him. Gary made the first two points of the second half from the foul line. After Gary made his second shot and was running back to get positioned in the half court 2-3 zone, Ronny Jay who was outraged and up in arms about being blown out by the Panthers, tried to punch Gary. With exceptional peripheral vision Gary saw the blow coming and he flinched slightly. So the ferocious punch Ronny Jay unleashed could easily have knocked Gary out if it had landed; only glanced off of his shoulder.

Gary unharmed, came up with the biggest grin of his life when he heard the referee blowing his whistle. He knew it was Ronny Jay's curtain call. Ronny Jay had fouled out of the game. At that point Coach Quinn stepped out onto the floor and was screaming at the referee who called the foul and was called for a technical foul. Ronny Jay went to the bench and sat down. His basketball career was over. All the Ashland fans were waving goodbye to Ronny and singing a chorus line from Roy Rogers' theme song, "Happy Trails to You."

Gary made three free throws in a row, and then he got to throw the ball in from out of bounds. Then the next fouls were called on Denny and Donny and they left the game. Then to round out the third period both forwards and the center for the Cougars fouled out. When the center fouled out Coach Quinn was so unhappy that he made the error of walking out onto the floor to argue with the referee a second time. This time Coach Quinn was called for his second technical foul and he was ejected from the game.

Gary thought it was the best thing that could have happened. Gary had a permanent grin on his face the rest of the game. Although Elm City had their starting center and forwards on the floor with fresh legs they were unable to do anything to stop Jack from scoring. During the break at the end of the third period Coach Hoff told Gary, "Jack has broken the school record, keep feeding the ball to him."

In the fourth period Gary had the game flowing to perfection. Ronny Jay was gone and so was Coach Quinn. Gary kept passing the ball to Jack. It was Jack's hottest night ever on offense. He was making everything go into the basket no matter from where, or what type of shot. He was in his sweet spot making hooks, lay-ups, jump shots, and he was deadly at the free throw line, everything went into the hoop.

The final score was Ashland 114, Elm City 46. Jack was the Tournament MVP scoring 51 points for the night. He put in 18 shots from the field for a total of 36 points, and made 15 free throws for 51 points to smash the school record and set the state record for most points ever scored in a Sectional Tournament in Illinois. Denny scored 17 points, Donny and Jerry both scored 16, and Gary contributed 14 points.

They were taking home their sixth first place tournament trophy for the 1957 basketball season. They had made it into the "Sweet Sixteen." Their record was 33 and 0. Only one other school in the state remained undefeated and that was Collinsville.

Ashland wanted to play Collinsville. They wanted to prove something to everybody in Illinois.

Gary never saw Ronny Jay or Coach Quinn for rest of his life. Ronny Jay never played basketball again, and about a week following their lopsided 114 to 46 loss to the Panthers the Superintendent of Schools over at Elm City fired Coach Quinn. He retired from basketball and found a new line of work in Elm City selling cars for Ronald Jay.

The Panthers and the Ashland community went wild celebrating all week end long. They were ecstatic and bubbling over with happiness. They were so proud of their basketball team. For Gary who finally gave Coach Quinn and Ronny Jay their comeuppance it was one of the happiest nights of his life.

The very next morning when the sun came up it hit him, "We're going to the Illinois State Finals," Gary shouted. Gary's pet parrot Humphrey began nodding his head up and down and he began to sing the new song that Gary had been trying to teach him all week, "By thy rivers gently flowing, Illinois, Illinois, and its mellow tones are these, Illinois, Illinois...." And Humphrey sang it over and over again.

True to his word Floyd Sorrells closed down the Elm City Café in the early afternoon on Friday for Gary's first game in Champaign. Floyd and Sea, his wife, and his son Mike came to pick up Gary's mom in their new station wagon. Gary's older sister Donna June was not living at home anymore. Donna had married a dairy farmer and moved to the country in Cherry Valley, up north near Rockford, Illinois. Another older sister Phyllis Joanne also had married and moved away. Her husband was an aircraft mechanic and they were living near a Top Secret Air Force Base out west. He was in the Strategic Air Command (SAC).

Gary's mom, Dee, and his younger sister Janie, and his little brother loaded into the station wagon with Floyd, Sea and Mike and the six of them headed for Champaign to watch Gary play basketball. It was a little more than a two hour drive. Gary's Aunt and Uncle Pete and Marguerite were going to the game and they had tickets so they would be sitting together.

In fact, almost everybody that lived in Ashland or in the countryside anywhere near the small community was driving over to watch the Panthers game. The downtown square of Ashland looked like a ghost town when the Panthers went to Champaign. They took five buses. The first bus was for the team only. The second bus was for the Cheerleaders, Band members and a few students like the Purple Panther mascot David Winklemann. The third bus was for students only. The fourth bus was for students and parents. The fifth bus was for fans; so that anybody in the community wanting to see the game could catch a free ride.

Trailing the buses was quite a caravan; more than one hundred cars were loaded with people from Ashland. The Panthers were prepared for their competition, a very big school from Chicago. It was a team that made regular appearances in the "Sweet Sixteen" nearly every year in the past decade La Grange High School. They were an exceedingly talented team.

Gary saw his family in the audience before the game. He was awfully proud that they had come to see him play ball and genuinely wanted to show them his best.

Jerry's sports report said, "In last night's game both La Grange and Ashland were nervous at the start. Both teams took bad shots and missed offensive rebounds, but Ashland settled down after Coach Hoff called a time out. In the first period the full court zone press baffled
La Grange. At the end of the first period the score was Ashland 20,
La Grange 4. In the second period La Grange figured out a way to break through the full court press and began to score. They were the first team all year to break through the Panthers press.

Coach Hoff shifted the defense to a man to man full court press. Then Jerry Conner was stealing the ball every time the La Grange guard had it. Jerry passed to Gary, who would dribble down and set up the offense, then he either passed it across court to Denny, or in to the big man Jack, either way Coach Hoff's 'Stardust Twins' were leading the way in scoring. They were proving to be the best one-two punch at scoring in the state. At the half the score was Ashland 48, La Grange 24.

In the second half Ashland stayed in a tightly packed 2-3 defensive zone. After ten minutes in the third period Wally, Glenn and Bob came in for Jerry, Gary and Donny, who sat on the bench until the period ended. La Grange had some excellent shooters, but Ashland never let down their offensive thrust and the score at the end of the third period was Ashland 76, La Grange 54.

Coach Hoff put Jerry, Gary and Donny back into the game at the start of the fourth period. La Grange made a strong run, but never came closer than within ten points. The entire second team played the final three minutes passing the ball around until La Grange began fouling. It didn't help because Ashland missed only one foul shot in the closing seconds of the game. The final score was Ashland 98, La Grange 88.

Denny and Jack were tied for high scorers with 23 points. Donny made 18 points, Jerry and Gary tied with 12 points. Everybody on the team contributed Wally had 3, Bob, Glenn and Edgar each made 2 free throws and Graham had 1 point. Ashland will play another tough Chicago team Saturday night when they face Westinghouse. At least the Panthers are playing these games on a neutral court. Fan support in Champaign has been great. Thanks to all the fans, we couldn't have gone this far without your support."

Gary's family was in the audience Saturday night and he had time to go up and say hello to everybody before the game. His good friend Jerry went with him. When the game began Westinghouse took the early lead. Ashland looked a little nervous at first, but Denny got hot and found his sweet spot, and he kept the Panthers in the ball game during the first period. The Panthers played in their half court 2-3 zone on defense and relied on Denny for offense. After the first period Westinghouse was leading 19 to 16.

In the second period the Panthers settled down and Gary got their run and gun offense rolling. It was a hard fought game with the lead going back and forth, but at the end of the half Westinghouse had regained the lead 42 to 37.

During the half Denny their team Captain said, "Westinghouse may be the best team we have played all year. We're in good condition; we can run with them and probably outlast them. Let's give it our best shot. I really think we have it in us to win this game.

Gary, turn on the steam out there. Let's go at them full speed. Let's show them just how fast and how good we are. When this half is over, then we will be in the final four and come back to finish the tournament next week. We have an advantage over this team. A couple of times tonight they were arguing with each other. We are all good friends; we know each other so well we can anticipate each others moves without saying a thing. Let's go out there and no talking until the game is over. Just concentrate on playing our best basketball. We are undefeated. They are not. Let's send them home to Chicago. I can see us making baskets, taking the lead, and winning this game. Win tonight and next weekend we could play Collinsville the only other undefeated team in Illinois."

Before leaving the locker room Jack put out his hand, the other players put their hands out on top of his and in unison they shouted, "Ashland Panthers, Go, Fight, Win!" And they ran out onto the floor to warm up. All eight cheerleaders and their mascot came out onto the floor where they were and encouraged them to keep fighting and not give up.

In the third period Gary made a couple of beautiful 40 foot left handed jump shots. They went up over everyone's head in an arch like a rainbow. Gary turned the offensive run and gun loose and slowly they evened the score by the end of the third period 53 to 53. Neither team would give an inch. They were both sprinting all out toward the finish line.

With four minutes left to go in the final period Coach Hoff gave the Panthers the sign from the bench to go into their full court press zone defense. Denny and Jerry double teamed the Westinghouse guard and Gary cut off his bad pass and bounce passed the ball to Donny who leaped up to about eye level with the rim and made an easy lay-up and they took the lead 62 to 60.

The Panthers continued to press and this time Gary stole the ball from the Westinghouse forward that he and Donny were double teaming. Gary turned away with the ball and quick as a flash he took it to the hoop. The score was 64 to 60. The Panthers continued the press. This time Denny intercepted the inbounds pass and went up for a jumper with out dribbling and swoosh—hit nothing but net. Westinghouse was stunned. Ashland had the lead 66 to 60, and with 1:57 showing on the game clock Coach Hoff called time out. He sat the starting five down on the bench and put in the second team.

Wally, Bob, Glenn, Edgar and Graham went in and the Ashland fans cheered wildly. They couldn't stop Westinghouse from passing the ball to their center and he scored easily. The score was now 66 to 62. But the Panthers had the ball out, and when they threw the ball inbounds, they went into a stall at the top of the key with all five players standing in a wide half circle passing the ball around. When the clock went down under a minute, the Westinghouse defense came out fouling to stop the clock.

Wally was fouled and he made both of his free throw shots. The score was 68 to 62. Then Westinghouse quickly passed the ball in to their center. Bob blocked his shot and after diving onto the floor and struggling with two other Westinghouse players Graham miraculously came up with the ball. The referees hadn't blown their whistles; they were going to let them play, and Graham immediately passed the ball to Edgar. The Panthers held the ball, completely unchallenged by Westinghouse, for the final thirty seconds until the clock ran out. The

Ashland Panthers had unbelievably pulled off another victory, and they were coming back next weekend to play in the final tournament.

The final score for the game was Ashland 68, Westinghouse 62. Gary was the leading scorer with 18 points closely followed by Denny with 17. Jack had 11, and Jerry and Donny tied with 10 points. Wally put in two free throws at the end for 2 points.

On Sunday evening Blondie Field and Charley Forman treated the entire basketball team and the cheerleaders to a banquet at the Springfield Airport Restaurant. Before the Banquet Wally gave an extemporaneous speech using facts Jerry Conner was gathering for the final sports article he was planning to publish after the tournament ended.

Wally said, "1957 has been an incredible basketball season worth remembering. But it's not over yet! Our team has broken all of our school's records. So far we have scored more points than any other year with 2,231 points. We have the highest scoring average making 75 points per game. We set both the highest game score with 114 points and the highest score by a player 51 points by Jack—both in the same game. We have been undefeated on our home floor two years in a row with 21 consecutive wins. Jack Lynn also has the record for most free throws in a game 15, with 75% shooting. We currently have 35 wins for the year without a loss, and if we can win the next two games we'll have a total of 37 victories in 1957. It has been a great season. This team wholeheartedly gives everything they've got when they are playing ball. We are going to have great and wonderful memories of this year to tell our grandchildren about. Oh what great fun it has been to be a part of this fantastic season. Next Friday night let's show who we really are and what kind of stuff we're made of when we are on the court. Then let's go on and take Collinsville to the wire and send them back home with their only loss in their final game against the 1957 Panthers."

On Wednesday evening at the close of their final practice, Coach Hoff said, "Well, the tough workouts have come to an end, but this season isn't over. I'm very proud of you all. It really is something... and I am honored just to have been able to know each one of you. I will never forget you, or this season of basketball. You have brought glory to the purple and white. Give these next two games 110%. I know we can win. Just go out there, do your best and have fun!"

Chapter 14

Floyd Sorrells closed the Elm City Café early, and drove his family and Dee and her children to Champaign to watch Gary play ball. Ashland was scheduled to play in their white home uniforms against Herrin High School, from Herrin, Illinois. But the first game was between Collinsville and Quincy. The Quincy Blue Devils had a great basketball team, but they were no match for Collinsville. Collinsville got out to an early lead and cruised through the entire game. The final score was Collinsville 72, Quincy 68. So Collinsville was watching the second game from the bleachers waiting to see who they would play against on Saturday.

Herrin took a 2-0 lead, then Donny Field made free throws to tie it up. Ashland had the lead 21 to 20 at the end of the first period. Herrin was going all out for a victory and had pulled to a seven point lead at half time Herrin 39, Ashland 32.

Ashland unleashed their full court press in the second half and turned on the steam. By the end of the third period the score was Ashland 60, Herrin 57. Herrin was an intensely stubborn team that fought the Panthers to the end. With ten seconds to go, Ashland had a two-point lead. Then, McCord made a last second buzzer beating lay-up for Herrin to send the game into overtime with the score tied at 81.

Denny Bast and Donny Field each scored in overtime to give Ashland the victory. Greenleaf had a chance to tie it up for Herrin on a 1 and 1 free throw, but he missed the first shot, ending the game with the score Ashland 85, Herrin 83. Donny Field was the Panthers leading scorer with 22 points. Jerry made 15 points, and Gary made 14 points. Denny made 12 points and Jack put in 10. Wally came off the bench to contribute 9 points and Bob added 3 points. The Ashland Panthers were in the final State Championship game against Collinsville. Saturday night one team would remain undefeated in the state of Illinois in 1957, and take home the First Place State Championship Trophy.

Saturday was a normal day for Gary. Excitement was in the air all over town, but Gary was calm and debonair. He had a fantastically good feeling about himself, his team and tonight's game, and he was ready to play his best game. He thought it would be incredible if one of the tiniest schools with the smallest senior class could win the state tournament. Gary was one of the poorest kids on the Panthers team, and there were many things that other kids had that they took for granted. He didn't have a car, his parents were divorced, and he had very little money. But what money he had, he earned and spent wisely. He didn't spend money on clothes for himself. He shared money with his mom and what he kept he spent on food and an occasional inexpensive movie.

Gary loved to eat and during his senior year he was well fed. Gary had learned how to cook and fend for himself and he ate some meals each week at his Aunt and Uncle's house. Gary wore two pairs of jeans all year to school. With them he usually wore a white T-shirt. He had a couple of shirts, but mostly he wore T-shirts.

Gary made the best of what he had. He had the gift of a great ability to understand sports. He loved to play basketball. Gary always had a sharp witted and light hearted sense of humor. He could make anyone laugh and usually did make his friends and family members laugh until it hurt. His friend Jerry actually thought Gary might become a professional comedian one day, he was that funny. He was gifted with an outstanding amount of natural talent and athletic prowess. He had speed, quickness and on the court he had prescient foresight. He had the ability to make you freeze with a look, a fake, and then he would drive around you to make a play, while you wondered how he did it. Quite simply, he was the kid that would beat you in basketball. He could find a way to win.

Gary was a kid who had every reason to think he was a loser in life, but he didn't. Deep down he had a burning desire to fight to the finish and come up winning. He knew he was a winner. Soon he would walk across the stage and receive his High School Diploma. It was the same stage his mom walked across. She had preceded him way back in 1930 when she was a young, beautiful seventeen year old girl and had her whole life ahead of her. Gary had his whole life ahead of him and he knew it. The study hall was the same place where they held graduation.

There were black and white photos all around the room of previous graduating classes that dated back to the 1880s. Earlier in the week the yearbook staff was going around taking pictures of students for the *1957 Echo.* A photo they took in the lunch room showed Wally at the head of the line and everybody at school lined up behind him for their hot home cooked plates of food. Everybody was happy. It was a normal school day frozen in time, but Elsie Buker the cook was aware the photo was about to be taken and turned her face toward the camera posing.

Another photo taken in the study hall that day showed all the students being studious and concentrating over their studies; also, in that photo Gary was at a desk reading a book; Jerry was at his desk holding a book too, but he had one hand on his chin and he was asleep! In addition, the yearbook staff took several club photos. Interestingly, Gary was in the Lettermen's Club photo. Gary was on the second row standing up. In front of him seated were the Varsity team and one JV player all wearing beautiful purple jackets with a big letter A (that stood for Ashland) on their jackets. Gary, of course, was wearing a white T-shirt.

None of those boys standing in the second and third rows owned a school letter jacket. Although Gary played high school basketball for four years he hadn't yet received a letter. Ultimately that was one of the reasons Coach Quinn in Elm City had been fired, because he had failed to award letters to several athletes who deserved them, and their parents had filed complaints in the school Superintendent's office.

Gary realized during his freshman year while living with his mom that he didn't have control over how some adults like Coach Quinn, or his own dad treated him; however, when the ball was in his hands and he was on the basketball court he felt very powerful and in control of the Panthers offensive attack. It didn't matter to Gary if he didn't have a school letter, or a lettermen's jacket to put it on. So what? He didn't let anything like that ever both him really. The nuances and awareness he had of those things, which were typically beyond his control, acted as a catalyst deepening his resolve to play harder, show excellent sportsmanship, and to always do his best.

Gary totally agreed with what Coach Hoff had told the team back at the beginning of the season. One day in practice Coach Hoff had said, "If a team beats us this year, hold your head high. At the end of the game shake hands, smile at them, and wish them well, because they had to be a great basketball team to beat you."

Gary wasn't worried about losing the game tonight. He just wanted to play well and to not let anybody down. He wanted to bring his best game to the floor, run and shoot as fast as he could and have fun. After that, let the chips fall where they may because tonight he would find out how great the Panthers were. Tonight's game would decide which team was the best basketball team in the entire state of Illinois.

Jerry walked to Gary's house, and then they walked together to school to catch their bus for Champaign. They knew tonight's game was their last and it would end their high school basketball careers. They really hoped to go out on top, with a perfect and unblemished record. They were in good spirits laughing and joking all the way to the bus. Uncle Pete shook hands with every Panther, just like he always did for every away game, as they climbed onto the bus. Uncle Pete stuffed a few dollars into Gary's pocket. Gary grinned and winked and said, "Thanks Uncle Pete....Thanks for bringing me back to Ashland to play ball."

"Have a great game Gary. I'm bringing Marguerite and we'll be in the stands after the game in the same place we were last time sitting beside your mom. Is Forrest coming?"

"Dad, are you kidding? He only comes to the home games, but he told me he'd be watching on TV." Gary said.

After the five buses were loaded up they drove away and another large caravan of fan's cars followed them all the way to Champaign.

In Elm City, Floyd and Sea Sorrells, along with their son Mike and all three of their daughters were piled into their new station wagon with Dee and her youngest son, and her daughter Sara. As they headed out towards Champaign Floyd said, "Dee we purchased a small gift for Gary. Win or lose he's had such a great season, we'd like you to give it to him after the Game. Sea picked it out."

"It was Floyd's idea. He noticed something he thought Gary would like. I had fun shopping for it though." Sea said, and her son Mike handed the present to Dee. Floyd was a very generous person, he was humble and sweet, everybody loved him and he was a great husband and father. He was the owner of the Café where Dee worked and he was the head Chef at the restaurant. Floyd was so over weight that he actually looked round, but he carried his weight well, and was such a wonderful person and great cook that nobody ever paid any attention at all to his size. Floyd had closed the restaurant four times in the past two weeks so that he could personally drive Dee to the games. That's the kind of employer he was.

When they arrived at the gymnasium they found it crowded with fans. This was the biggest most important game Ashland would play in 1957. Dee sat down beside her sister Snig who was already there to watch Gary play basketball. Pete and Marguerite had brought a picnic basket with more than enough sandwiches, fruit, snacks and drinks to share with everybody they were with at the game.

Collinsville was undefeated with 33 wins this season and Ashland was undefeated with 36 wins. This game was a close call, but the Chicago sports writers were giving Collinsville a seven point edge. Excitement for the coming event was contagious in the gym.

Fans had been arriving for two hours, and both teams were inside the locker rooms dressing. Ashland was selected to wear their home court white uniform with purple trim. Coincidentally, Collinsville's school colors were the same as Ashland's so they were wearing purple uniforms with white trim. There was an ocean of purple color in waves across the stands. Collinsville's team mascot was a Native American Chief in full headdress and they were called Kahoks, (pronounced Kay-hawks) from an authentic native tribe indigenous to Illinois. The Panthers had been waiting all year for an opportunity to play the Kahoks.

Collinsville had played in the final state championship game for three consecutive years. Last year Herrin had beaten them by one point. The year before that, they had won the state tournament. In fact, the Kahoks had three state tournament victory banners hanging from their home court rafters. Tonight they were planning to count coup against the Panthers.

Coach Hoff knew how to use intimidation to their advantage. They had to look like a good basketball team; that's why they wore short hair, sharp uniforms with their shirts tucked in, knee length socks with a wide purple stripe at the top and knee pads. They always came charging out onto the floor running at top speed and circled the court dribbling basketballs, and then Jack and Donny would dunk the basketball while the rest of the team put in lay-ups. Tonight when they came out onto the floor, they were wearing their new purple warm up suits for the first time, and they looked impressive.

The game was being broadcast statewide on Channel 4 TV and was being broadcast across Illinois, and far beyond, by WLDS-FM Radio. The gym was packed with standing room only. Tickets were less than a dollar and relatively inexpensive. The Ashland High School Student and Alumni Band were seated above the tunnel. The Kahoks Band was at the opposite end of the gym. As the Panthers ran onto the floor for warm ups the band played the Harlem Globetrotters theme song, and the crowd roared.

The Panthers had a set of routine drills they did for 20 minutes before the game to warm up. They went through their exercises, stretched and practiced a few shots. Then they took turns making free throws. The Collinsville Kahoks did the same on the other half court, and then both teams ran back under the tunnel. The Kahoks starting players were called by name one-by-one, into the spotlight and they dribbled out as they heard their names. Then the rest of the Kahoks came out and went to their bench. Then the Ashland starting five was called out into the spotlight one-by-one, they also dribbled out, as their names were called, and then the rest of the Panthers came out, and went to their bench.

These two teams had never played each other before. Jack and Denny went out as co-captains to meet with the Kahoks co-captains and the referees at the center of the floor. When they came back the cheerleaders and team mascots ran onto the floor to lead cheers. At that point the Ashland Band played the Notre Dame Football fight song and all the Ashland fans sang the Ashland school fight song.

> "Cheer cheer for old Ashland High!
> Loyal we'll be until we die!
> Send a volley cheer on high!
> Shake down the rafters from the sky!
> What though the odds be great or small!
> Old Ashland High will win over all!
> While her sons go marching, onward to victory!
> Rah...Rah...Rah...!"

At the tip-off Jack tipped it to Donny. Donny threw it back to Jack who scored. On the next play Gary intercepted the ball being passed to a Kahoks guard and tossed it quickly back to Jack who put it in, and the Panthers took an early 4-point lead.

Everybody on the floor still had their pre-game jitters though. Players on both teams knew they were in for the toughest battle of their lives. Purple uniforms with white lettering seemed to be everywhere the Panthers looked on the floor. The Kahoks came on strong and the Panthers were really feeling pressured from the game, the fans, and their undefeated season. They knew they were playing against the same team that had played in the last two state championship final games, and it really began to hit the Panthers hard.

Everybody in Ashland was rooting for them. Most of their pressure was self-imposed because the Panthers really wanted to win. Jerry was tense and probably was trying too hard. In this very important, tight, close game, he made a lot of early fouls. Jerry had always felt shadowed by Jack and Denny, and they were great ball players. Jerry had an inferiority complex and under the pressure of tonight's significant game his problem reared its ugly head. Jerry, who had always been shorter than most of the other boys, and had always worn thick lensed glasses that made him feel bad, lost his normal calm and confident demeanor in the game and played over aggressively.

Gary played like the Panthers' old teammate Dick Edwards; only tonight he was better, and the Panthers were a better team with Gary's help. Although the score was even for most of the game, the Kahoks began pressuring Ashland and were gradually taking control of the game. As the clock wound down toward half time, the Kahoks were gaining confidence and building a lead. Jerry and Gary both were scoring well and contributing to the team effort to stay in the game.

Gary leaped 38 inches up and tucked his legs way up underneath him. From about 45 feet away from the backboard Gary released his beautiful left handed jump shot like he had all season long. With accurate follow through and his left hand extended the basketball went up with reverse spin arched like a rainbow, fell down through the hoop with a loud swoosh, hitting only net.

Bob McCarthy the team manager was sitting on the bench beside the coach performing his clipboard and shooting statistic duties. When he saw Gary's jump shot he turned to the coach and said, "That was the most beautiful left handed, jump shot with a follow through that I've ever seen."

"I'm glad Gary's on our team, not playing against us." Coach Hoff said.

After making a basket Gary scooped the ball away from the Kahoks point guard and snapped a pass to Donny. He was about eight feet from the center line when he caught Gary's pass and immediately he threw a no look pass to Jack who made an easy dunk. The crowd went wild cheering for the play. Coach Hoff called a timeout. During the timeout the whole team congratulated Donny for his great no look pass to Jack, and Donny really felt great.

The game was so closely contended that every pass, every free throw and every shot was going to be important. Back in the 1950s they didn't keep statistics on assists, if they did then Gary and Jerry would have set several records for assists. When Donny made that pass it sent the crowd into a frenzy; that was the first time Donny had ever noticed the crowd was cheering for him. It made him excited to be in the game.

During the timeout while the Kahoks were trying to regroup and plan their next strategy all eight of Ashland's Cheerleaders: Janet Buker, Gloria Gerdes, Bev Plattner, Barb Buker, Sharon Forman; and the JV squad: Carol Gerdes, Lynell Field, and Elizabeth Wright, including David Winklemann the Purple Panther Mascot, all went onto the floor to lead two cheers.

PURPLE AND WHITE, FIGHT, FIGHT, clap! clap!
PURPLE AND WHITE, FIGHT, FIGHT, clap! clap!
WHO FIGHTS? WE FIGHT! clap! clap!
PURPLE AND WHITE, FIGHT, FIGHT, clap! clap!

And their next cheer went like this:

GIVE US A P....P
GIVE US AN A....A
GIVE US A N....N
GIVE US A T....T
GIVE US AN H....H
GIVE US AN E....E
GIVE US A R....R
GIVE US A S....S
WHAT'S IT SPELL?
PANTHERS, Louder
PANTHERS, Louder
PANTHERS!

Donny felt great coming out of the timeout. There were just a few seconds remaining in the half. The next time the Panthers had the ball the half time clock had nearly expired. Jerry tossed the ball in to Gary who immediately threw a baseball pass to Donny. Again Donny was about eight feet from the center line. As time ran out Donny released a hook shot and the ball came off the glass backboard rolled twice around the rim and went in and tied the score 35 to 35. Again the whole crowd of Ashland fans cheered wildly for Donny, and Donny never felt better. It was the best moment he ever had playing basketball. The whole team was congratulating him as they went into the locker room. Donny was having the best game of his life. The crowd continued cheering wildly for Ashland as the team disappeared into the tunnel.

Chapter 15

It was an incredibly exciting first half of basketball. At half time Donny went into the locker room feeling like he had just experienced the best half he had ever played. He was on cloud nine. Jerry went in feeling exactly the opposite, he felt like it was the worst half he had ever played, and to make matters worse for him, he felt awfully bad because he thought he had let everybody down. Jerry never felt lower than at that moment. Jerry sat in the locker room discouraged because he had already committed four fouls.

It was a tough hard fought half. Jerry had banged up against a Kahoks forward and came away with a bloody nose. It happened underneath a backboard. Jerry took off his glasses, and wiped the blood off onto a mat that was hung against the wall to prevent the players who ran into the wall from being injured. After wiping the blood off onto the mat Jerry put his glasses back on and went back into the game. He was one tough guy. Later on during a timeout he told one of the players on the bench, "I know what I was thinking. I've got to stop this bleeding or the coach is going to pull me out of the game, and I don't want to come out." Jerry had a difficult time. It was one of those games where after every bump and bang from a Kahoks player, a foul was called against Jerry. In the first half Jerry did not have one opportunity to go to the charity stripe.

During half time Pete ate a sandwich and enjoyed sitting in the stands with everybody. Normally if the Panthers were on their home court he would be down on the floor pushing a dust mop. He was impressed by how well the Panthers had played.

Marguerite gave out drinks and sandwiches and snacks to her sister and her children and to the Sorrells family. And they enjoyed listening to the bands that both played at half time.

In the locker room Coach Hoff tried to give his team his best positive psychological motivation. He told them they were doing great. "Keep applying the pressure and you will win. Give it 110% the team that will win this game is the one that gives the best they have. This can be the best half you will ever play. Focus individually on doing what you do best to help the team. I know you will win."

The teams came out of the locker rooms and the crowd cheered. After they took some warm up shots they huddled around their team benches as the Panthers Cheerleaders went out onto the floor.

S—U—C—C—E—S—S!
THAT'S THE WAY YOU SPELL SUCCESS!
WHO SHALL HAVE IT?
CAN YOU GUESS?
NOBODY ELSE BUT A—H—S!

The Panthers cheerleading outfits were long purple skirts that came down half way between their knees and ankles. They wore white turtleneck sweaters with AHS in purple across their chests, and white tennis shoes and socks with purple tops rolled down. The band wore all white with purple capes, and purple hats with large fluffy white plumes on top.

The Purple Panther Mascot danced beside the Cheerleaders as they performed their cheers.

2—4—6—8!
WHO DO WE APRECIATE?
THE TEAM, THE TEAM,
THE WHOLE DARN TEAM!
3—5—7—9!
WHO DO WE THINK IS MIGHTY FINE?
COACH HOFF!

As the second half got underway the Panthers knew the going would be tough; that half would make or break one of these team's perfect season. Gary displayed impressive speed on the court and was good dribbling and shooting. He could hit a 15-foot jump shot from anywhere around the basket. When Jerry brought the ball up court he'd pass the ball to Denny who would score. Once in a while he would shoot, or pass it to Jack who would make a basket.

When Gary brought the ball up he did much of the same. Once in a while he would shoot, but only if he felt the team needed a boost. Ninety percent of the time he'd pass it away. He was great at faking a shot, then getting the ball to an open man. Usually that was Denny or Jack according to Coach Hoff's regular offensive plan. Gary would pass the ball to anybody that was open though, and with his great peripheral vision he could see the entire court, and he always knew where his team was when they were in the game.

In the second half Gary found his sweet spot and everything slowed down and everybody else seemed to be playing in slow motion. Gary's teammates were always ready for him to pass the ball. Everybody knew Gary threw quick passes when they were least expected, but they always caught his passes. All of Gary's teammates were excellent shooters.

Coach Hoff did not pull Jerry Conner out of the game. He liked to let his starting five play. His philosophy was—if you have received your fourth foul, then you simply backed off defensively. Wally was his best sub on the bench and Coach Hoff would put him in as a guard or a forward when a player fouled out. Occasionally he would go to Bob Savage, but he was confident enough with his bench to let a player foul out. All of the players were in tremendous physical condition.

A few minutes into the third period Jerry fouled out of the game. The team would really pull together now because they had lost one of the best guards in the state of Illinois. Jerry never had a chance to shoot one free throw the whole game; every call went against him. Every effort was made by the team from that point on to shore the game up and win. Coach Hoff sent Bob Savage in to replace Jerry; he decided to finish the game with one point guard, three forwards and a center.

In the huddle Gary said to Bob, "Relax, have fun and get into the rhythm of the game. I'm not going to pass the ball to you—so watch for me to fake a pass every time. I'll let you know verbally when I'm going to pass to you, ok?" And Bob nodded.

"Denny, Jack, Donny, watch out for the ball." Gary said.

The weight of running the offense fell solely into Gary's capable hands. That responsibility and pressure made him step up the pace and turn on the steam. The Kahoks had built an 11-point lead for themselves. When Gary brought the ball up the court he faked a pass to Jack and went up for a two-pointer at the top of the key. From that moment on he only passed the ball, or faked a shot and then passed the ball to Denny, Jack and Donny who turned on the steam and made several important baskets.

The Collinsville Kahoks had scrappy players and excellent shooters as well. Four of their players were already shooting in double figures, and three of those: Knuppel, Harfast and Jockish had 19 points or better. They were going to fight to the very end trying to defeat the Panthers.

Finally, with 2:30 left in the fourth period the Panther's fast break at a breakneck pace began to wear on the Kahoks. The Panther's tied the score at 66 to 66. Gary who had been passing only to Denny, Jack or Donny all through the entire half said to Bob, "Watch for the ball, and take a shot." Their full court zone press worked, and Denny got the ball and passed it to Gary. He brought the ball up the court and set up the offense. He began to drive, and then he faked a pass to Jack, then to Denny, and snapped a pass to Bob who was wide open. Bob put in an incredibly easy lay-up and the Panthers had taken the lead 68 to 66.

Immediately, in the blink of an eye, Jockish ripped a long jumper and tied the score again 68 to 68. Gary sprinted dribbling the ball with blistering speed and bulldog tenacity straight toward Donny. That meant for Donny to come up and set a screen on the purple uniformed Kahoks guard. Then, "the old screen and roll," Gary dribbled around the screen, Donny turned and ran toward the basket.

Since the time that Jerry had fouled out Gary had been passing the ball and had only shot one time. He was trying to guide and direct the flow of the offense toward the easiest and best percentage shots so the Panthers could win the game. Gary was left unguarded, and that time instead of passing to Donny, he was going to take what he thought might be his final shot.

It was exactly the way Gary wanted it. It was magical. It was perfect. With less than 20 seconds on the game clock Gary stopped his dribble, sprang up 38 inches with his feet neatly tucked underneath him. At that point, there was a hush in the crowd, and silence filled the gymnasium. It was magical. Gary released another shot. It was the most beautiful, backward spinning left-handed over the head jump shot anybody had ever seen. It arched 15 feet up and came down with a swoosh that was heard throughout the whole gym as the ball ripped through the net. The crowd went wild as Ashland went ahead of Collinsville 70 to 68.

But the game wasn't over yet. The never say die Kahoks rapidly threw the ball up court without dribbling and got it into the sure hands of Jockish, who made the basket quicker than the Panthers could believe. That tied the game at 70 to 70. The Panthers pushed the ball up court with blazing speed trying to get another basket before time ran out, but the Kahoks took the ball away and raced to the other end of the court.

With only two seconds left on the clock the Kahoks passed the ball into the sure hands of Jockish. As Jockish went up for the shot and released it, the game ending buzzer sounded, the ball fell through the hoop hitting nothing but the net. The Ashland team and their fans were stunned; it looked like they had lost the game. But the referee blew his whistle and said the shot didn't count because Jockish had released the shot a split-second after the buzzer had sounded. If he had released it before the buzzer sounded then it would have counted. The game ended with a tied score 70 to 70. They would play basketball five more minutes in overtime.

Now the moaning and groaning of the first few weeks of Coach Hoff's conditioning program came into the minds of all the Panthers. The Panthers were ready to play on. Their opponents were beginning to look worn out and haggardly. In the overtime Jack tipped the ball back to Denny who passed it to Gary. Gary fired it up to Jack as soon as he was set, and Jack made the basket. The next time the Panthers had the ball Gary again threw it to Jack, but Jack was fouled. He made both of his free throw shots.

When they went back on defense Jack attempted to block a shot by Harfast and fouled him. Jack had fouled out. Wally came into the game as a guard and Bob shifted over to Donny's forward position, and Donny moved up to play center. Right after Jack sat down when the Panthers got the ball again Gary dribbled up the court exactly the way he did when Jack was in there, he headed toward passing the ball to Donny. He faked a pass to Donny and fired a pass across to Denny who he saw open. Denny put the ball up and in with the same steady precision he always had on the court, and the score was 76 to 72.

Collinsville came down the court and Harfast made two more points for the Kahoks. Ashland went into a stall and the Kahoks decided to come out and foul Bob. It was an intensely hard fought game all the way and both teams continued to battle in the final seconds. Bob made his first shot at the charity stripe bringing the score to Ashland 77, Collinsville 74. Bob missed his final free throw and Knuppel came down with the rebound, too late, and the clock expired and the final buzzer went off.

The Ashland High School Panthers won the 1957 Illinois State Tournament 77 to 74. The fans cheered and celebrated. Gary and Jerry and everybody on their team hugged each other. They waited in line to shake hands with the Kahoks and tell them what a great game they had played.

Gary and Jerry were the last of the Ashland players to climb up the ladder and cut down the net. First Jerry went up and Gary held the ladder and then Gary went up while Jerry held the ladder. While Gary was up there taking the net all the way down Jerry shouted up to Gary, "What are you going to do next?"

"I'm going to Disneyland!" Gary said, with wink and a grin.

After he climbed down Gary ran up into the stands to find his family.

Denny was the high scorer with 22 points, and Jack was close with 21 points. Donny made 14 points, and Gary made 11 points. Jerry made 6 points, and Bob made one timely basket and one free throw for 3 points. Denny Bast was the tournament MVP.

In the stands Gary hugged his mom, sister and little brother.

"You were great." Gary's mom said.

Everyone was excited and happy. Gary's mom gave him his present and he opened it up. It was a purple Ashland Lettermen's jacket.

"Now you have something to wear your Varsity letter on." Floyd said.

"Wow this is fantastic! Thank you!" Gary said.

He wore the jacket back down onto the gym floor and sat down beside Jerry. Jerry said, "Seriously Gary, what are you going to do next?"

"Well....I might take up golf." Gary said, and then he smiled.

A few minutes later, the Panthers had their photos taken joyfully holding up their 1957 State Championship trophy. They had won thirty-seven games and retired undefeated.

Donny Field became a Chicago High School math teacher, coaching basketball and baseball.

Jack Lynn became a Vice President for a bank in Springfield.

Denny Bast became a printer for the Journal Register in Springfield.

Jerry Conner became a Mass Media Law Professor at the University of Wisconsin.

Gary Pearn became a General Manager for Scotties Home Improvement Company, Orlando.

www.ingramcontent.com/pod-product-compliance
Lightning Source LLC
Chambersburg PA
CBHW030824310726
48980CB00006B/629/J

* 9 7 8 0 9 7 7 7 3 1 8 0 0 *